WHERE THERE'S SMOKE, THERE'S LIARS

WOKE ISLAND BATTLE ROYALE

RANDOM

MOUSE

RANDOM

MOUSE

WHERE THERE'S SMOKE, THERE'S LIARS

WOKE ISLAND BATTLE ROYALE

ALEKSANDËR EATON

For Sal

TABLE OF CONTENTS

"Your 'truth' and 'the truth' are not the same, even though you have designed your life around the idea that they are."
—Gary John Bishop

"If we cancel everyone who ever makes a mistake or has an unpopular opinion, the only voices left are those of liars."
—Chlamydia Vestibule

"If you're not cancelled, you ain't really poppin'."
—Tamika Mallory

"Tyranny is the deliberate removal of nuance."
—Albert Maysles

"As far as I can see, cancel culture is mercy's antithesis. Political correctness has grown to become the unhappiest religion in the world."
—Nick Cave

"The mob was fed lies."
—Mitch McConnell

"Freedom is what we do with what is done to us."
—Jean-Paul Sartre

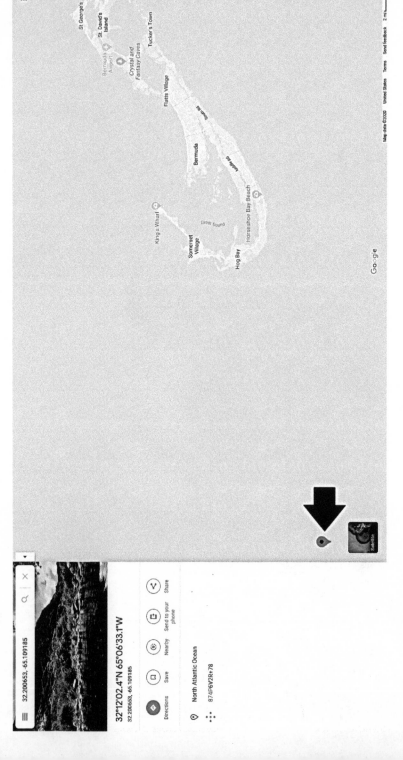

32°12'02.4"N 65°06'33.1"W

32.200653, -65.109185

Directions   Save   Nearby   Send to your   Share
                                    phone

North Atlantic Ocean

874P6V2R+78

WOKE ISLAND

Zippo	Diary & Pen	Compass
Chopsticks	Canteen	Watch
Hunting Knife	Multi-tool	Duct Tape
Toilet Paper	Flashlight	Hatchet
First Aid Kit	Whistle	Mirror
Dildo	Ball Gag	Fleshlight

PART I:

BEFORE
THE
ISLAND

In my dreams, I kicked them down long flights of stairs.

In my dreams, I caved in their skulls with a hammer.

In my dreams, I punched them till my hands were bloodied, and their faces were unrecognizable.

In my dreams, they admit they have lied with the express purpose of destroying me.

In my dreams, I send them each a little note that simply reads, "You won't know where, and you won't know when."

In my dreams, none of this ever happened.

People asked, "Why didn't he respond to the allegations?" Well, lemme ask you this: If you were walking alone in a park, and hundreds of people mobbed you, beat the living fuck out of you—punching you till you fell to the ground, then kicking you while you were down—would your first move as they dispersed be to get back up immediately and start wildly swinging at them, knowing that they'd all just fall on you again and continue attacking? Or would you stay curled in a fetal ball until they'd worn themselves out, and had left the park—at which point you could slowly get up and drag yourself home to lick your wounds?

Every lawyer and PR firm I contacted told me to do the latter—which I did. "In our experience," they said, "if you starve the fire of oxygen long enough, it will go out."

Eventually, everyone did leave the park. I picked myself up from the ground, dusted myself off, and limped home.

Oh, and by the way, more than half the people

kicking you while you were down had—until earlier that same day—called themselves your friends.

◊

Now imagine that a plane carrying 200 people crashes, and you knew everyone on board. You're never going to see them again. And they all blame you for the plane going down.

◊

You have no idea how fucking tortured I am about whether to call this book *Where There's Smoke, There's Liars*, or *Where There's Smoke, There're Liars*. However, the subtitle, *Woke Island Battle Royale*, was never in doubt.

◊

Alright, alright, maybe time to back up some, and tell you what this is all about, yes?

I *was* going to launch into the full nitty-gritty here, but then I realized there's no need. You've seen the story in the news a thousand times by now. Once something is said on the internet—especially on social media—it's seen as true unless proven otherwise. And even if it *is* proven false, it won't matter much—as a character in the show *The Great* once said: "The first lie wins."

People—close friends, hangers-on, and complete strangers—told horrendous lies about me. One lie snowballed into another, everyone jockeying for title of Most Woke.

After the first spark caught, and I saw the beginnings of the outrage pile-on, I deleted my social media accounts immediately, and never went back on. (I only know what was said due to concerned friends and family.)

Shit went from bad to worse.

I nearly killed myself one night. The only thought that saved me was: *I can't. No one will be here to feed Warble.* (Warble is my dog.)

It's only now, five years later, that I can write about it.

NEWS FLASH: I have the internet, too. If I chose to weaponize it against these vicious fools how they've weaponized it against me, none of them would remain untouched. Not a single one.

How well do they think their dirty laundry would fare, being hung up to dry on the clothesline of the internet? Stripped of context, stripped of nuance, stripped of *their side* of the story?

I have said for years that the left will eat itself, but I never realized just how mindlessly *hungry* it is.

It is the death of dialogue—the only thing standing between peace and war. But the ferociously woke *want* war. They *want* to cancel, tear down, delete everything they don't agree with. In their eyes, the time for dialogue is over. Theirs is a singular vision—born, quite ridiculously, of postmodernism and neo-Marxism—in which you are either with them or against them. "Silence is violence." And there is no middle ground. There is no place to stand to discuss differing viewpoints. All one needs do is look at the current state of the world to see that we are all just shouting our beliefs at each other. Our opinions siloed in echo chambers, reverberating back to our eyes and ears from a hundred or a thousand similar voices on our screens, all bellowing the same thing. Shouting down anyone who offers a dissenting view. Shaming all who dare to disagree.

There are two types of people in this world—and this is a new distinction, one that was never before been possible, but now is, due to the advent of social media, which connects and distorts the entire planet: There are only those who have been shamed, and those who have *yet* to be shamed.

The human brain is not designed to process this sort of thing. I don't think it has evolved to deal with the sheer scale of a social media pile-on involving *hundreds* of people. It's only been during the last handful of years that we've seen these events happening to more and more people—and for more and more ridiculous reasons.

There're three responses the brain experiences when threatened: fight, flight, or freeze. I experienced all three of these at once. I wanted to retaliate; I wanted to disappear; and I wanted to just sit still and do nothing in the hope that I would wake up from what I perceived as a true living nightmare.

I lost my job, my reputation, and 90% of my "friends." Got the locks changed. Kept the blinds drawn day and night. Didn't go out, didn't answer the phone, dreaded the mailbox. Kept waiting for a knock on the door to deliver even more horrendous lie-based news.

For the first two weeks, each morning my alarm would go off, and there'd be that second or two of normalcy—my mind booting up to start dealing with what used to be a regular day's work—then the reality of the situation would throttle me, and I'd remember what had happened, and that it was all real, that it wasn't going away.

That I would never again wake up to my old life.

It wasn't long after this two-week period that my defenestrators started vanishing.

Cletus-Jo Horsegrazer (the names of the guilty have been changed to randomly generated hillbilly or whimsical fairy names 'cause why not have some fun with one's ruination?) was the first to vanish without a trace. More would follow, but he was the first.

Sorry, should I have mentioned that earlier? Yeah, a bunch of these people went missing, and I was arrested as the prime suspect.

More on that later!

Married couple Tammy-Lou Sheepchaser and Jerry-Ray Barngreaser were the second and third people to vanish. There didn't seem to be any rhyme or reason to the order in which people were disappearing—and I told the police as much when they brought me in after the fourth of my defenestrators, Cloverdrop Snowmint, couldn't be found. "Honestly," I told them, "I'm as baffled as you guys are about all this." Naturally, they were a tough sell, considering what the people vanishing had done to me. But it was the truth. I didn't know what was going on, and was legitimately as confused as the cops.

I use the word "confused" because, unlike other disappearances the police were used to investigating, there wasn't a shred of evidence as to what had happened to those who'd gone missing.

No witnesses saw them get abducted. No evidence of scuffles. Nothing amiss in their apartments or houses. Nothing on their social media accounts or in conversations with their friends that might indicate they were under threat, suicidal, etc. No large amounts of money taken out of bank accounts. No weird credit card uses. No odd cell phone calls.

Nothing.

Just *poof.*

Gone.

But hang on, before I get to the vanishings, while we're talking about online *performances,* can I tell you my favourite thing about this entire horrorshow?

When it all got shanked, the contact form on my website remained open for months. And while the attacks piled up online—on blogs, in the news, on social media—*not a single piece of hate mail came to me personally.* Not by email, not by text, not by telephone.

Why, you may ask, would that be the case?

Because sending personal messages via email doesn't score you any social cred. If you send an email, no one gets to see how woke you are, how much a champion for all that's good and right you are! You need to pile on in full view of all your compatriots so they can *see* with their own eyes that You Are On Their Side, and that You Are One of Them.

No point virtue signalling to the person you're trying to shame, is there? That's wasted time, wasted pixels. Best to put those pixels to use on social media where the whole world can see that you don't agree with the things those mean people did, the terrible things they said.

Since The Before Times—which is how I've unofficially come to think of everything prior to the day things went to shit—it's been over five years, and I still haven't received a single individual piece of hate mail.

My email address didn't change.

My text number didn't change.

My phone number didn't change.

The only thing that's changed with the advent of social media is that everyone's hatred has become *intentionally* public. Personalized hatred is useless in the race to become the most victimized, the most bullied, the most disadvantaged, the most *put upon* in the world. How are you expected to get all those dopamine-driven Facebook likes and Twitter hearts for "speaking your truth" if you have to do it one stupid fucking email at a time?

Come on! Get your shit together! Post your wildly inaccurate/context-free accusations online, and watch the sympathy flood in! Your followers will increase! Your woke cred will skyrocket! Evidence be damned—evidence is for boomers! Nuanced arguments are boring! Just put on your crime-fighting underwear, and let 'em have it!

Have an axe to grind with someone regarding an issue completely unrelated to the thing you're about to accuse them of? Don't overthink it! Just post the most damaging thing that comes to mind. You will be *believed*, so why hold back!?

And even if you're forced to one day retract your lies, no one will notice or care at that point—the damage to the person you hate will have been done, and you'll just carry on with your life, free of consequences!

I often wonder when these people get up in the morning—especially those who claim to be the shaming victim's close friend—do they wash one face with the left hand, and the other face with the right hand?

We live in the conscienceless liar's paradise. You can say whatever you like, and no one is allowed to question you. Prior to the advent of social media, you wouldn't be able to ruin someone's life on this scale without needing to convince the police, a lawyer, a reporter—hell, someone, *anyone*—of your grievance.

Giving a voice to the voiceless is only good when it's used to tell the truth. And, contrary to popular opinion, there *is* such a thing as *the truth*. This idea of "your truth" is one of the most dangerous ideas to come out of the last decade. It leaves no room for logical argument, dissenting views—a path forward to common ground. You cannot discuss, argue, or have any meaningful dialogue about someone's situation when they're able to shut down criticisms by invoking the notion of *their* particular truth.

If every person on earth has their own truth, what can possibly remain of humanity's shared experience?

The first three disappearances all took place on this continent, but Cloverdrop lived on another continent altogether—I think that's why the cops weren't as hard on me as they could've been when questioning me. I guess they realized that any case they might have against me was falling apart now. There was really only the kidnapping-for-hire angle, since the time frame—about three days from Cletus-Jo's disappearance to Cloverdrop's—dictated that it wasn't physically possible for me to have kidnapped all four people.

When the fifth through eleventh hillbillies/whimsical fairies were nowhere to be found within the space of about four days, the cops let me go because, no matter how baffling the situation was—and how clearly tied to me in at least *some way* it seemed to be—you can't hold someone for kidnapping seven people while he was in police custody.

The twelfth through twenty-third people vanished even more quickly than the first eleven, but by then I was at home in Marrakech, reading about it online, the cops having given up on my involvement, left with no witnesses, no evidence, nothing on which to hold me.

By the way, if you find yourself "triggered" (O, buzziest of woke buzzwords, how I loathe thee!) at any point in this book, please consider as a first course of action *closing the book*. You'll find that will solve the problem more quickly and efficiently than expressing your outrage about the book's content on social media.

And in a much less annoying fashion for those around you.

By the way, part 2: Even if I'd done the terrible things they said I did—which again, and for the goddamn record, I absolutely did *not*—how is this a societally acceptable way to handle it? How is shaming people online actually addressing the problems society faces?

If anything, all this has done is made me *much* more centrist in my political views—and I used to be as hardcore left as you could imagine. When the left starts acting like the right in its intolerance, the centre is the safest place to hang your hat. Hell, maybe the *only* place to hang your hat. Although, even on that front, a friend of mine said, "It's not *you* who's changed, it's the left that has changed." Both sides are so rabid now, it's sometimes impossible to tell who's who.

The sad thing is that now whenever I hear about a celebrity supposedly sexually assaulting someone, or bullying them, or saying offensive things about minorities, etc., I'm *much* more skeptical, given what I've been through, not to mention the percentage of complete bullshit involved in my case. I used to simply *believe* like everyone else, but now when I hear these stories in the news, I think, *Well, maybe it's true—or at least some of it— but what other axe is there to grind in this situation? What's the other side of the story? We don't know what's gone on between these two people. Maybe the accuser just hates the accused for unrelated reasons—bad blood between them for years—and with the advent of social media, this is a tried and true way to ruin someone without getting a speck of dirt on themselves—thanks to the poisonous shame-happy milieu we currently inhabit.*

The broader the definition of all these terms becomes, the easier it is to ruin people's lives. What used to be thought of societally as racist, transphobic, misogynistic, etc., last month is not how those terms are perceived this month. The goalposts perpetually shift. It's like a minefield the left initially created for the worst of the right, but with more and more mines added every day, the left inevitably winds up blowing itself to pieces.

By the way, part the 3rd: Guess what, you children disguised as adults: The world isn't a safe space. For 98% of humanity, it's a constant fucking struggle.

But it's because of mass rape, genocide, poverty, war— not because someone looked at someone else in a suggestive manner, or because a man tapped a woman on the shoulder in a queue because she didn't hear him telling her the line was moving again, and that was somehow a patriarchal microaggression—and so now let's take a picture of him and post it on Twitter because he needs to lose his job. He needs to be cancelled.

Do you really think that will turn him to your "side"? Have you reactionary knee-jerks even thought five minutes into the future about this? Or is it all just about "accountability"? A great word in a lot of cases to disguise one's unhinged thirst for revenge.

I suspect more often than not, all shaming that guy will do is send him straight into the arms of the extreme right, where he'll find an understanding, a kinship—a common opinion that this bullshit has gone too far. But instead of cogent dialogue, all you'll get in return is a feedback loop of hatred.

Some socially awkward nerd puts his arm around you at a party because he misread the signals, so it's time to take that easy target to *pieces* online. Really ramp up that social cred you've been cultivating, right? Never mind that his small misstep gets him shitcanned from work and ruins his reputation.

I've actually heard the following as rationale for this abysmal behaviour: Some eggs have to be broken to make an omelette.

So, in this analogy, the omelette is social equality, and the eggs are the fucking people whose lives get destroyed *for no good reason* along the way?

Oh, and what of intention? This idea that intention doesn't matter, only outcomes matter.

A bigger pile of horseshit I can scarcely imagine.

Picture this, if you will:

Only one plane crashes into the World Trade Center on 9/11. The tower it hits still crumbles, and the exact same amount of lives are lost. It is later revealed that it was due to pilot error, computer malfunction, or a combination of both. Is this the same as terrorists hijacking the plane and slamming it into the building with the *intention* of murdering thousands of people?

Only a dullard would think these two situations are

morally identical—or a disingenuous bad-faith actor with a narrative to further at all costs.

If you see these two situations as identical, I would posit that there is something malfunctioning with your neural pathways.

There's a reason the law has varying degrees of responsibility for killing someone. If you meant to do it, it's murder; if you didn't, it's manslaughter. And this sliding scale applies to every single interaction humans experience.

Intention absolutely fucking matters.

But I digress.

Let's get to the Island.

Wait! I forgot one more thing. The bright, blinding sun of that tropical island where all our heroes' dreams come true —paused in perpetual sunshine—can wait one more moment.

I'm a determinist, so I don't believe in free will; I believe free will is an illusion.

You did not choose to be born.

You did not chose your parents.

You did not choose your nationality.

You did not choose the environment into which you were born.

You did not choose your sexual orientation.

You do not choose what happens to you throughout your life based on that predetermination coupled with random chance.

You do not choose what to think next. You have no

control over what pops into your head at any given moment. Neuroscientists have proven that your decisions are already locked in roughly seven seconds before you're aware of what you're going to do. You think you're making a decision of your own "free will," but all you're doing is what has already been predetermined by your genetic make-up, past experiences, environment, etc.—everything that has led you to the given moment in which you're about to make that next decision.

Existence is merely a series of cause-and-effect events, one leading to the other, stacking atop one another like earth strata, and this includes every molecule in your body. Every strand of DNA. Every neuron.

I do not believe—with perhaps small increments of deviation—that you can choose what you do with your life, the next year of your existence, the next day, the next breath.

Everything in consciousness is merely arising, and you are reacting to it, based on the deterministic star stuff of which we are all made.

In my dreams, I kicked them down long flights of stairs.

In my dreams, I caved in their skulls with a hammer.

In my dreams, I punched them till my hands were bloodied, and their faces were unrecognizable.

In my dreams, they admit they have lied with the express purpose of destroying me.

In my dreams, I send them each a little note that simply reads, "You won't know where, and you won't know when."

In my dreams, this is the only way things could have turned out.

PART II:

THE ISLAND

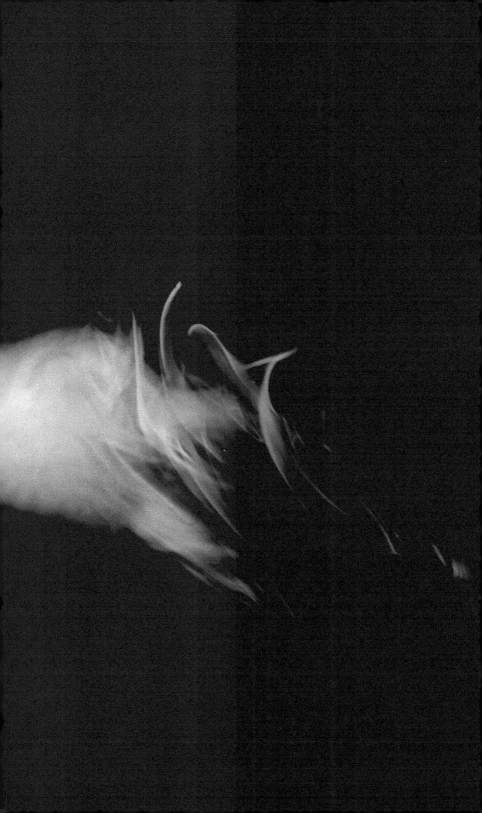

Somehow—I have no idea how, but somehow—all twenty-three of the people who wronged me the most egregiously wound up in one Maersk shipping container together.

Even though they'd disappeared at different times, they apparently all just popped into existence in the container simultaneously—there were no witnesses to any of them getting into the container, and the security footage on the dock corroborated that fact.

They just vanished from their normal lives, maybe hung out in some existential waiting room in another dimension, then—when the Time was Right—they all just poofed into the shipping container.

They would eventually wind up stranded on a very small Bermudan island—one of the 123 little islands in the region. For you geography nerds, the precise location was 32°12'02.4"N 65°06'33.1"W in the North Atlantic.

The only theories I've been able to come up with for how it happened are these two:

1. I blacked out, repressed my memories, and hired professional kidnappers—so good they eluded all witnesses and security cameras while spiriting away twenty-three people from several different continents in the space of a couple of weeks.

2. I subconsciously *willed* them into the shipping container. Mysterious and unbelievable as fuck, I agree, but given the facts, I'm not sure what else to think.

The container was blue with white lettering, and had only sat on the dock for about twenty minutes with everyone inside before being loaded aboard a container ship headed from Montreal to Jamaica.

There's no record during those twenty minutes of how they reacted—even the group's intrepid diary-writer, performance-vegan and gluten "sufferer" Dixie-Ann Goatbaler, didn't have the presence of mind (or the light, I guess) to take notes—but I'm gonna take a flyer and say they were freaked the fuck out.

Each person was *transported* (or whatever) to the container carrying one item. Over the course of their adventure, we'll find out what each person's special item was.

Exciting, no?

Yes!

Dixie-Ann's was her little diary, which luckily had a tiny pen attached, so I guess the metaphysical travel agent responsible for their trip let it slip on a technicality as a single item. But yeah, it woulda been pitch dark in there and, what with all the presumed panic at suddenly finding themselves locked in a shipping container, it's unlikely that Moontouch Jellypuff (delighted husband of Honeydance Flitternose) would've realized his item was a Zippo lighter.

Okay, so we'll assume they're all freaking out—especially when the container starts to move as it's slowly loaded onto a ship—but likely taking some comfort in the fact that they recognize the desperate/shrill/panicky voices around them. A lot of them are friends, and they're all at least tangentially aware of everyone else in there. Especially since a bunch of them came together to take me down.

Old home week!

The container settled on the ship with a massive metal clang.

Silence.

Darkness.

Heavy breathing.

Then: "Oh my god," Jodi-Lynn Cangbritches said. "Who just brushed my arm?"

(Dixie-Ann related this first upsetting episode in woke paradise during her first diary entry—dated a few hours after they wound up on the island.)

No one said anything.

"Well, *someone* just fucking brushed my arm. Who was it?"

More silence.

"Look," a male voice, Dicky Cowherder, said. "We need to calm down and try to figure out what's going on here, okay, Jodi-Lynn?"

Jodi-Lynn fell into what can be assumed was a sulk. She probably didn't pursue the alleged arm-brushing incident because she didn't know what was going on, or for how long they'd all be trapped together. Plus, she likely reasoned she should save her strength for future outraged allegations surely in her near future.

"Wait," another male voice said, this one Amos Gigglesheen. "Dixie-Ann and Jodi-Lynn are both here, right?"

They both answered yes.

"Well, I always get you two confused—maybe because of your hyphenated names, I'm not sure—so let's go by last names for you guys."

"Oh, sure," said Jodi-Lynn. "Let's just bow down to the patriarchy, and let the *man* tell us what names we're allowed to have. Sounds about right, doesn't it? Besides, you *do* know that there are a bunch of us in here with hyphenated names, right? Or is it only the women you can't tell apart? Also, what is this 'you guys' shit? Just more fucking patriarchy. Big surprise."

No one could see inside the container, but it's safe to assume Amos, being terrified of stepping wrong in any way, shape, or form, was blushing, and probably stammered when he replied, "That's not what I meant, no, sorry. I would never try to minimize your truth, or your experience, or . . ." He was floundering, and the two women were eating it up. They lived for this kind of awkward squirming. They felt it balanced the power dynamic between the sexes.

"Save it, Gigglesheen," said a third female voice, Emmy-Lou Piddlintater, joining the conversation. "If Jodi-Lynn and Dixie-Ann have to go by their last names alone, so do we all. Or had you planned to bring your white male dominance of the world into this container, as well? Two names for men, one name for women? If there was a kitchen in here, would you have us barefoot and pregnant in it? Should we make you a fucking sandwich?"

Gigglesheen was definitely not going to say another word now. Piddlintater was black—the only black person in the container, as a matter of fact. *And* a woman. Anything he might say in response would be mansplaining. Worse yet: *white mansplaining.*

So he just shut his mouth.

Wise move, Gigglesheen. Wise move.

It would likely come as a surprise to Piddlintater that— as pointed out by Glenn Loury, RuinedLeon, Coleman

Hughes, Gothix, John McWhorter, Africa Brooke, and Candace Owens (before you swoon onto your fainting couch, have you actually listened to her speak *at length* about this issue, not just a cherry-picked sound bite?)—not all black people consider themselves victims of existence.

Jellypuff then got up a bit of nerve (he was a little older and crustier than the others), and said, "We shouldn't argue. We don't know what's happening here. Arguing will only make whatever lies ahead for us even more difficult."

Since there were ten women and twelve men, the gender representation was just about evenly balanced. There were murmurs around the container. Half sounded low, the other half a bit higher, so at first blush, perhaps a consensus had been reached.

No fighting, if they could help it—at least until they knew what was happening. Of course, that might be easier said than done because—even though they'd all come together to crater my life—there was plenty of bad blood between them:

Goatbaler hated Merle Pigscouge, talked all *kinds* of shit about Trigger Mudherder, positively *detested* Horsegrazer, and said the most horrendous mean-girl shit about Cangbritches.

Cangbritches loathed Jellypuff and Horsegrazer. Jellypuff was forever getting Cangbritches' pronouns wrong, and she never forgot that he didn't "like" her post when she announced on social media that she was pansexual.

Honeydance Flitternose called Snowmint disparaging names behind her back, usually in reference to her body.

Or her face. Or her personality.

Bart Gumphook Jr. was certainly no fan of Horsegrazer, describing him to close friends as "materially and socially worthless."

And *hoo-boy*, do Barngreaser and Sheepchaser ever have a hate-on for Cowherder. All sorts of rotten blood going on there, having to do with a deep dark well of nasty shit too long and sordid to get into here.

But these paragons of morality and kindness should *absolutely* be the arbiters of what everyone else thinks and feels, shouldn't they? They've set the bar, for sure.

Careful not to trip over it.

"Is there, like, even enough air in here? Aren't these things, like, um . . ." Cangbritches was having trouble with her words. "Whaddaya call it? Hermuntically sealed?"

"Hermetically sealed," Jellypuff replied. "And that's not mansplaining, just regular *ex*plaining. Honest."

Cangbritches wanted to say something nasty back, but she couldn't think of anything, so she just rolled her eyes in the darkness.

"And no," Jellypuff continued. "They're not hermetically sealed. Depending on the cargo, some of them have vents. Hopefully this one does."

"Okay, Professor Shipyard. Sorry for asking," said Cangbritches. It was the best she could do under these tense circumstances.

That's when Jellypuff patted his front pockets at a strange shape he felt there. He pulled out the Zippo. Flicked it.

Light flooded his section of the container. Everyone gasped like our first hominin ancestors must've over a million years ago.

"Ugh," Cangbritches said when she saw Jellypuff's face. "It was better when we couldn't see you."

Jellypuff knew better than to respond.

Even in a shipping container, the threat of public humiliation was a real concern—what if Cangbritches' one free item turned out to be a cell phone? Twitter and Facebook were only a finger-tap away!

They didn't know yet that they'd all been issued said free item, but when they found out, you could be sure they'd be jealous of whatever the other people got.

"Well, I don't know whose lighter this is, but it isn't mine," Jellypuff said. "Anyone else wind up with something in their pockets that doesn't belong to them?"

The faint sound of rustling as people poked around in their pockets. Sure enough, everyone had an item they didn't recognize.

A rippling murmur ran through the unwilling container-mates. What could it mean? Where did these things come from?

"Okay, hang on, simmer down," said Scooter Fishstench, who was used to being listened to. He had a strong voice, and was full of himself, so people listened. If you have a strong, clear voice, you can spout all manner of bullshit and still be taken seriously. He had also proven himself to be an uber-ally by taking down several of his friends online recently, so he was currently riding that particular wave of woke-cred. "Did anyone get a pen and paper, or anything we can write with? If so, we'll catalogue what each person has, so we can pool our resources, see what's useful to the situation."

The most woke in the container were torn about

whether to follow Fishstench's instructions because, yes, he was speaking common sense, and he *did* have all that recent woke-cred in his back pocket, but at the same time, he was a cisgender heterosexual male, so . . . toss up.

But in the end, no one challenged him on this. Fresh woke-cred for the win.

Jellypuff flicked on his Zippo. The light infused the container.

This is when Goatbaler discovered her diary/pen combo. "I have something to write with, and a little diary!"

"Great," said Fishstench, who then pointed to the back of the container, and said, "Alright, let's start with Pigscouge, and we'll work our way toward me. Just state what you found. Goatbaler can write it down.

Pigscouge: "Compass. And chopsticks. Guess I'm special; I got two."

Beau Corntrigger: "Water canteen."

Fishstench interrupted. "Wait, you found a whole water canteen in your pocket?"

"No, but it was at my feet, so I assume it's meant for me."

Fishstench nodded, but made a mental note to keep an eye on this Corntrigger guy. Water is a valuable commodity in any uncertain situation. If he's got the only canteen, he may have to be shamed into relinquishing it. And there was no one better for the job. Hell, if shaming didn't work—it was less likely to when the audience was only twenty-two other people with no access to the internet—then a solid beating would have to suffice. Fishstench sized Corntrigger up in the dim, flickering light from Jellypuff's Zippo. Seemed in good shape, but a bit thin. Doubtful to be a problem.

"Alright, keep it going," Fishstench said, relishing the command in his voice. This is how you slowly become the group leader. Just take charge. Unearned confidence will trump most wishy-washy introverts in a heartbeat.

Flitternose: "Watch."

A beat.

Then Cedardance Twirlfluff said, "Watch what?"

Several people groaned.

"No," said Flitternose, an edge to her voice. "I found a watch in my pocket. As in, a *time-keeping device.*"

Piddlintater: "Hunting knife."

Ricky-Boy Chickenpicker: "Multi-tool."

Mudherder: "BOOM!"

Goatbaler said, "Ugh, stop it. Just answer the question."

Goatbaler knew—as did a few others in the container—that Mudherder always signed his emails with "BOOM!" Annoying as hell. I guess he was trying to brand himself? Who knows.

Anyway, after sulking for a few seconds, he finally answered: "Duct tape."

Before the next person said their item, someone whispered, just barely audibly: "Maybe we can use that duct tape on Mudherder to make him stop fucking saying "BOOM."

There was giggling.

More sulking from Mudherder.

But people should be careful; this was treading dangerously close to bullying.

Molly-Jean Dirtplanter: "One roll of toilet paper."

Twirlfluff: "Emergency flashlight. One of those wind-up kind."

Gigglesheen: "Hatchet."

Piddlintater mumbled something about whitey getting the best weapon, of course, but everyone ignored the quip, and just waited for the next item to be read aloud. There would be plenty of time to attack each other for all sorts of perceived slights later.

Fishstench: "First aid kit."

"Whitey gets to heal first, too," grumbled Piddlintater.

Fishstench ignored her, and just said, "Next."

Hank-Bob Hoghauler: "Plastic whistle."

"Like a rape whistle?" asked Flitternose.

Hoghauler was a cisgender heterosexual white male—like nearly every male in the container—and he didn't want to step wrong here. He blushed, and said, "I'm not sure. Could be? I suppose it could be used for anything you want to alert people to, so . . . yes?"

I suppose I could have gone with "Jellyspine" instead of "Hoghauler" for this character, but too late now.

"Well, shouldn't that go to a woman, then?" Flitternose responded.

Fishstench took charge again, said, "We'll discuss who gets what after we do the inventory. Please, let's just get through this."

Right then, something sounding like a massive boat engine began thrumming beneath the container.

"Looks like we're heading out shortly, folks. Let's speed it up," said Fishstench.

Snowmint: "Mirror. Like for hygiene or, I suppose, signalling in a pinch."

Horsegrazer: "Water canteen."

Sheepchaser: "Canteen."

Barngreaser: "Canteen."

Daisy Willowbell: "Water canteen."

Harlan Stinkberry: "Same."

"Wow, lots of water. Good to know," Fishstench said. "Did we miss anyone?"

Gumphook, Cangbritches, and Cowherder wouldn't meet Fishstench's eyes. They just stared at their feet, and shifted from side to side.

Everyone gave a little gasp as the background thrum revved up more, and the cargo ship pulled slowly out of port.

"Well, we're on our way *somewhere*, I guess. Jesus," said Barngreaser.

"Come on, spill it," Fishstench said, pressing. "What do you guys have?"

Cowherder was the first to crack: "Dildo."

Lucille Gristlespoon: "Same."

"Wait," Fishstench said. "Gristlespoon's here, too?"

Gristlespoon is Cowherder's wife. She stepped out from behind Cowherder, where she'd been standing the whole time.

"It's okay," she said. "No one ever sees or hears me because I'm tiny, and I'm a woman."

Someone groaned.

Cangbritches: "Ball gag."

"Excuse me?" Gristlespoon said, clearly affronted.

Cangbritches: "Not for you. I have a ball gag. That's my item."

Gristlespoon would have to wait for another opportunity to be mildly victimized.

Gumphook: "Fleshlight."

In a less woke shipping container, the last three items

may have elicited some juvenile laughter, but no one wanted to be singled out for inappropriate behaviour, so everyone remained silent, internalizing their laughter for fear of offending someone.

You may only find humorous what the consensus of the woke mob has agreed you're *allowed* to find humorous. I'm actually surprised no one called out Gumphook for even *knowing* that he was holding a Fleshlight.

The woke mob would love to go through your browser history to judge whether your taste in porn is diverse and inclusive enough.

With the awkward moment passing—no one knowing where to look, clearing their throats, etc.— Fishstench broke the silence: "Well, everything's useful, I suppose, and our benefactor clearly has a sense of humour, foul as it may be."

The machine sounds around them had levelled out to an even chugging thrum. They were well underway.

"So, no food?" asked Pigscouge.

"Yeah, that *is* worrisome," Fishstench said. "Let's do a sweep from front to back, make sure we didn't miss anything. Nice and slow. Look everywhere."

They did a slow sweep.

Nothing. Not even a box of racially problematic Cream of Wheat.

"Might I suggest," Jellypuff said, "that we check to see if there *are* actually vents in this container? If we're going to be in here for a while—and it certainly appears that way —we'll need to know how much air we can reasonably expect. Then take actions to make that amount last as long as possible."

Barngreaser voiced his agreement. Jellypuff and

Barngreaser were the least woke in the container, and were known to adhere fairly faithfully to logic and reason— two of postmodernism's greatest enemies—and they were friends, so this was an alliance worth keeping a close McCarthy-esque eye on.

"I'll hoist you," Barngreaser said. He was quite tall, so it made sense for him to hoist the much shorter Jellypuff.

Jellypuff passed his Zippo to Cowherder. "Keep it lit while I'm up there, and just try to shine it as high as you can."

Barngreaser interlaced and cupped his hands. Jellypuff stepped one foot into them, pushed off from his back foot, and Barngreaser lifted, held him up as high as he could. Jellypuff felt around with his hands flat against the metal. "Ah! Found a vent."

A collective sigh of relief issued throughout the container.

Barngreaser let Jellypuff back down. Cowherder closed the Zippo, passed it back to Jellypuff. "Yeah, we should conserve this. Twirlfluff's flashlight is better since it won't run out, so long as one of us has hands to crank it up."

Gumphook tried for a joke: "Unfortunately, my *Fleshlight* doesn't give off much of a glow." He looked around with a little smile.

The joke fell flat, and everyone just turned away from him.

As people began chattering amongst themselves, speculating what was happening, what it all meant, Cangbritches suddenly said, "OMG, it's, like, a sex-trafficking ring."

And yes, she said the initials OMG, not the words

"Oh my god."

Someone gasped—there were a lot of gaspers in this crew.

"Um, look around you," Flitternose said. "I mean, some of us could be desirable for sex-traffickers, I suppose, but . . . well, not to put too fine a point on it, but we're not exactly the age range. Or the . . . um, fittest bunch?"

Careful, Flitternose. Tread lightly on this.

"Oh, are we going down this path, Flitternose. Really?" asked Pigscouge. "Really?"

"Look, I'm just saying, the odds that this is a sex-trafficking ring are pretty slim because—"

"*We're* not?" Jellypuff interjected.

That actually got a few chuckles, which were quickly stifled before anyone could recognize the chortlers in the dark.

"Well, either way," said Snowmint, "what are we going to do? Just sit in here until we get to wherever we're going?"

"You have a better idea?" asked Barngreaser. "Maybe a blowtorch you smuggled in that you neglected to tell us about?"

That quip seemed to knock the sauce out of everyone.

A silence fell over the container, and everyone shuffled to an area to be alone, or found a friend to pair up with.

Someone muttered something about getting some sleep —they may all well need it for whatever came next.

The cargo ship rocked ever so slightly back and forth on the waves. Comforting. Lulling the weary travellers into the gentle hands of slumber.

Time passed. People nodded off.

Most were oblivious to the danger they were in. Nothing like this had ever happened to them before, and they just assumed someone would help them. The police. Maybe someone on board the ship. Surely this couldn't stand.

Weren't they *owed* more than this by life?

As sleep loomed closer, a couple of people briefly raised the notion of yelling for help, cursed themselves for not thinking of it earlier. But others pointed out—between yawns of exhaustion—that it was extremely unlikely that anyone would hear them beyond the solid metal walls of their container, the thrum of the engines, the wind, and the waves slapping rhythmically against the hull of the ship.

Probably right was the consensus on that point.

Sleepy people were much easier to convince than wide-awake, panicky people, so this line of thought, appropriately, went nowhere.

Two hours passed, maybe more.

Then a shrill voice in the dark: "Get your hands off of me!"

Jellypuff flicked on his Zippo. Twirlfluff wound up her flashlight.

"What happened?" Fishstench asked, wanting to reassert himself as the group's leader/saviour. "Is everyone okay?"

Cangbritches was sitting up against one of the container's walls, where she'd been trying to sleep moments ago. "Someone grabbed me! I felt hands on me!"

Chickenpicker, who was seated not far from Cangbritches, blushed and said, "Well, I *was* feeling along the ground in the dark to try to locate my multi-tool, and if I accidentally brushed up against you—"

"Oh, accidentally? Yeah, right," Cangbritches said, crossed her arms, and glared at Chickenpicker.

Everyone in the container knew that Chickenpicker was the *last* guy in there who would try to sneak a grab in the dark, but no one stuck up for him. They all just sat silently, and waited to see how this would play out.

"I'm really sorry, Cangbritches. I honestly would never try to—"

Cangbritches cut him off, screeching: "You don't *get* to apologize! You're the abuser, and you don't have the right! I don't care what you 'intended'! What matters is how you made me feel!"

Chickenpicker blushed even deeper, opened his mouth, contemplated making another attempt at a sincere apology, to try to explain that his intention had not been to touch her, but to simply locate his multi-tool in the pitch-black darkness.

In the end, with Cangbritches glaring at him, and the rest of the container seemingly indifferent to his plight— self-preservation being a stronger force than loyalty, or even any sense of decency or notion of friendship—he bowed his head, and said nothing at all.

Chickenpicker shifted his body several feet away from Cangbritches, and kept his head down.

After what seemed like a decade, Twirlfluff's wind-up flashlight wound down, and merciful darkness enveloped the container again.

The container inhabitants slept for a few more hours, then woke to a stifling heat, seemingly cooking them where they sat. Even though there were air vents, the amount of people in the container, and the direction they were headed—toward Jamaica—made it more and more likely with each passing day that they'd simply roast to death.

There was the usual sniping that second day, too, but with less gusto, and people separated into groups.

The day passed mind-numbingly uneventfully.

The third day was more of the same. Goatbaler barely wrote in her diary after day three, except to note that people were at least being kind with the water rations, but testiness was starting to become real anger since there was no food—and no one knew where they were headed, so they had no clue how far along their trip's path they were.

Day four came and went.

Day five. A fistfight nearly broke out between Corntrigger and Hoghauler—best friends in regular life, but just two starving, dehydrated humans stuck in a giant metal can now.

Day six. Fewer tempers flaring as hunger took its toll on their energy.

Day seven:

The day of the storm.

A clap of thunder woke the container. Horsegrazer actually yelped as the sound rattled him out of a fitful slumber.

The trip to this point had been fairly smooth—the occasional big wave would slap the side of the boat, but other than that, the weather had been calm.

Tonight was a different story entirely.

Thunder shook the container. Rain pelted against the metal, not only from above, but from the sides, as well. The waves slapped the hull much stronger than before. The din of everything combined made it difficult for people to hear each other, even those seated right next to one another.

Jellypuff was the first to comment on what everyone was suddenly thinking about. He said, "I hope the lashings hold."

"That's a cheery thought," said Barngreaser.

"I kinda hope the lashings *don't* hold," said Stinkberry. "At least it'll be a change from this godawful day-after-day sameness."

"Yeah, at least until we sink to the bottom of the ocean," said Chickenpicker.

"Which will happen very fast, since even without anything inside these things, they weigh tons," said Gumphook.

"Well, look at us, all coming together to chat about our impending demise in a watery grave," Jellypuff commented. "But we won't necessarily sink."

Just then, a particularly massive crack of thunder assaulted their eardrums, then rumbled across the sky. The storm was right above them.

Another wave crashed into the boat, and this time, they actually felt it heave to one side.

"Holy shitsnacks," said Hoghauler. "That's not good, you guys. What do we do if the boat sinks, or those lashings *do* come undone?"

"In both cases, we're fairly fucked, so no need to worry," Jellypuff answered unhelpfully.

Another gigantic crack, and it sounded like the sky had split open directly above them. Rain now hammered the container so forcefully that when Cangbritches, Goatbaler, and Horsegrazer screamed, no one heard them.

If you scream in a shipping container, and no one hears it—including yourself—did you even really scream at all?

The next wave that slammed into the boat knocked the container to one side.

"Uhhh, that actually felt like we lifted *off* of whatever we're *on*," said Flitternose. "How well are these things secured? Does anyone know how they do it—like, really *know* what the procedures are, and—"

"Oh, I don't know, 'Karen'," Twirlfluff said—referring, of course, to (as Wikipedia states) the 'pejorative term for a woman perceived as entitled or demanding beyond the scope of what is appropriate or necessary'—"would you like to speak to the fucking manager?"

Another tremendous, sky-splitting crack interrupted Flitternose's question, then another wave plowed into the side of the ship.

No one would get to ask any more relatively calm questions for a while after this because that last wave would knock their container—and the two beneath it—into the ocean.

When the container hit the water, everyone started screaming and shouting. People ran from side to side, up and down the length of the container, desperately—and against all reason—looking for a way out.

It was complete chaos.

Even Fishstench and his commanding voice was of no help.

Weakened by hunger, and with the water canteens getting worryingly low, the panicking only had so much energy in it, and could only last for so long. Everyone also quickly realized that sitting down—braced either by another person or a container wall—was the best way not to have your skull cracked open.

For the first few minutes, the wind and waves buffeted their container against the other two containers that'd fallen off the ship—the sound of the giant metal quadrilaterals crashing and scraping against each other eliciting screams, moans, and beseeches to a god in which most of them didn't believe.

Once the waves had separated the containers, and it was just the sound of the storm and the waves, people settled down a bit. There were still mutterings of useless prayer, and the occasional bout of cursing, but even that stopped after a little while.

The background thrum of the cargo ship receded.

The darkness in the container seemed to be a living entity—smothering everyone's speech. No one said a word. There was simply breathing. No one even asked Jellypuff to flick on his lighter, or Twirlfluff to wind up her flashlight.

They seemed content with the darkness.

"Guess we're not gonna sink, after all," said Jellypuff.

No one took much solace in the fact.

The storm raged on for another hour or more. Who could tell? Time had ceased to matter. Evenly distributed as best as possible, the container-mates finished off the last of the water.

What did it matter anymore? So hungry and dehydrated, some felt that dying would be a mercy at this point.

But that sweet relief was not in the cards for this group.

Moments after Mudherder lifted a canteen over his head, mouth wide open to catch the last droplets, the storm picked up again—more thunder, stronger winds.

Those susceptible to sea-sickness had so far been able to hold the contents of their stomachs down, but this new wave of buffeting was too much, and several people threw up on themselves and others. Those whose barf didn't get soaked up by flesh and clothing saw their noxious contributions sloshed about on the container floor.

The sight and smell then caused others to throw up, the result being reminiscent of the Mr. Creosote scene in *Monty Python's The Meaning of Life.*

Someone may have also shit themselves.

No one offered up a confession, but the smell was unmistakable, and could have issued from no other source than between the cheeks.

Pigscouge began to weep openly—great heaving sobs. She wailed and slammed her open-palmed hands into the puddle of puke between her legs, which splashed up into her face and peppered across her thighs. Inconsolable, she bellowed, "What did we do to deserve this!?"

What struck me most when reading this passage in Goatbaler's diary was the naivete of thinking that people get what they deserve.

Just then, an enormous wave slammed into one side of the container, lifted it up so that it was very nearly airborne, and dashed it against a massive sea stack. The tremendous force of the wave that tossed the container into the rocks rent open one corner of the container in an ear-splitting, jagged tear.

Everyone was tossed up and dashed against the opposite side of the sea can.

Water flooded in, but so did sand granules—not that anyone would notice that until they'd regained consciousness.

Everyone had been knocked senseless except for the five people who died on impact—two of them gashed open and split apart on the thick steel of the container tear.

Emmy-Lou Piddlintater died with no visible wounds. Investigators later said her head just crashed against a particularly thick section of the container, and it was instant lights-out.

Daisy Willowbell met a similar fate.

Lucille Gristlespoon's head was caved in, but investigators concluded she did not suffer . . . much.

Harlan Stinkberry was one of the two tossed into the jagged steel of the rip—he'd been partially decapitated by the sharp, bent-in metal as his body passed through the opening to land on a shallow part of the shore where the water and sand mixed fairly evenly. Investigators would later say that if he'd only suffered the neck wound, he might've lived for another thirty seconds or so, but the water and sand found in his lungs showed that he'd been doubly doomed.

And finally, Corntrigger: The jagged strip of metal that'd nearly decapitated Stinkberry on his way out now sprouted from Corntrigger's back, plunged cleanly through his chest.

The storm began to calm now, as though these five deaths had been sacrifices to the gods.

And they had accepted.

Several hours later—the storm having completely passed—the sun rose over the horizon to shine on one of the 123 little islands near Bermuda. If Stinkberry were standing up and alive on the shore of this island—instead of face-down dead in the water, his head hanging half off his neck —he would not be able to see any of the other small islands in the area. The survivors were far enough away from any other land masses that it seemed as if this was the only island in the world.

And again, assuming Stinkberry hadn't become fish food, and had been capable of sending up a camera-drone for a bird's-eye view, the picture retrieved would show a lovely calm beach, pristine blue water, through which you could just about see right to the bottom, peppered with sea stacks—one of which, particularly close to the shore, had a shipping container lodged against it as it baked anew in the sun.

Blood in the water.

Goatbaler was the first of the survivors to awaken.

Shaking the fog from her mind, she looked around the container, saw what appeared to be five dead bodies, and quickly did a calculation.

Five bodies for eighteen people, she thought. She did not know where the thought came from, but she was adapting to her new environment. She reasoned that if they were, indeed, stranded on a desert island with slim hope of escape, they would be forced to cannibalize the dead.

Her mind began churning, while her stomach did the same.

She looked down at her diary/pen combo. *Not much use for carving up a body. . . . Wait, who had the knife again?*

She got slowly to her feet. Her body ached from being thrown around the container, but nothing seemed to be broken.

As she approached the corpses—confirming her initial assumptions by checking pulses—she walked past Gigglesheen's prone form where he still lay unconscious, snoring away. She remembered he had the hatchet.

Yeah, but he's still alive, she thought. These thoughts were disturbing her because she wasn't fully aware where they were leading.

She spotted Piddlintater's corpse, saw that the knife was not too far from where she'd landed. Goatbaler glanced behind her quickly to see if anyone was looking, but no one else was awake yet.

She reached down, picked up the knife, carefully slid it in her waistband, turned around, and went back to the spot where she'd woken up.

She closed her eyes, and the math appeared in her head, unbidden:

Five divided by eighteen is not even a third of a body—how long can a person last on one third of a body? If we had five more, that would be, what . . . over half a body each. But wait, no, even more than that because those five people would be gone, too, so it'd be ten divided by thirteen, which would be over three-quarters of a body each.

She was excited by this idea, but also horrified at the fact that her mind was already working in this fashion. Maybe they'd get rescued. Maybe they weren't that far away from another island. Maybe the shipping vessel they fell off would alert the Coast Guard or someone else, and they'd find them. And even if they did have to spend a lot of time here before any rescue happened, maybe they wouldn't need to resort to cannibalism; perhaps there'd be plenty of fish, or perhaps the island had boar on it, or lots of edible plants. Who knows?

But deep down in her subconscious she knew that was all fairly unlikely. Based on their luck since inexplicably being abducted and stuffed into a shipping container to begin with, whatever the universe had planned for them, it was probably not going to be pleasant.

But hang on, hang on, hang on, she thought, literally giving her head a shake, standing up quickly now, and pacing in a small circle. *I have to get hold of myself. This isn't me. I'll just grab Gigglesheen's hatchet as added protection, and do a quick survey of the island—or of however much I can in a short time span, depending how big the island is—and see what*

I see. I mean, sweet Jesus. Let's put cannibalism on the back burner for as long as we can.

Goatbaler walked over to Gigglesheen, looked around the area, spotted the hatchet; he was partially lying on it. It stuck out halfway from under one of his thighs. She quietly reached down, gently pulled it out from under his leg.

He didn't wake. Didn't even flinch.

Again, she was unsure why she was tiptoeing around, not wanting to wake anyone up. All she knew was that instinct was telling her to do this—that, at least for now, it was better for her situation if everyone remained asleep.

Armed with the hatchet in one hand, the knife in the other, she dropped the little distance between where the container was lodged against the sea stack and the bloody sea where Stinkberry's body bobbed, his head occasionally knocking against the metal of the container, sounding a dull bonging noise in time with the gently lapping waves.

The water was only about waist-deep.

One last glance inside at the occupants of the container, then she waded the few feet to dry land.

Standing on the shore, she breathed deeply of the salty air, glanced up at the sun where it glared down high in the sky.

Nothing moved on the watery horizon. Behind her, nothing moved in the trees comprising what looked like a dense forest.

Another disturbing, unbidden thought got her feet moving: *Hurry up. Those first five bodies won't last long in this heat.*

She headed quickly toward the forest.

Goatbaler had barely gone about two hundred metres into the forest when she thought she glimpsed water on the other side already. *Can the island really be this small?* she wondered. The trees had been thick when she'd entered, but had quickly thinned out, then grew thick again as she continued another hundred feet or so.

She came out the other side of the forest to find another beach, nearly identical to the one upon which they'd been dashed in the storm. Sea stacks peppered this side of the island, as well. It appeared as though they ringed the entire tiny island.

What is it, maybe five hundred metres the way I just walked and—from what I can see—another 500 metres crosswise, for easy math? So, like, a quarter of a square kilometre?

Not that she was an expert on islands, of course, but she'd been expecting something perhaps *Lost*-sized. Somewhere you could really tell a great mystery—lots of hidden caves, a lagoon, maybe.

Disappointed, she glanced down the beach, and saw—near where the sand met the trees—a small pool. She ran toward it, convinced it would be a mirage when she arrived, just like in countless movies.

Although no one would ever call it a lagoon by any stretch of the imagination, it was a sizable pool of water. But was it fresh water?

She dropped to her knees, cupped her hands, thrust them into the clear depths, drew them back, pulled them up to her lips, and drank. The moment the water was in her mouth, she knew it was fresh.

She gulped it down.

Back for more. Gulped that down, too.

When she'd had her fill, knowing not to take too much or she'd be sick, she noticed that the ring of rocks around the pool seemed to purposely demarcate it somehow.

As though it was man-made, she thought.

But, of course, that was silly. All the way out here? Wherever *here* was?

But the thought stuck.

She had to admit, it was very convenient that a lovely little fresh-water pool just *happened* to be on this tiniest of islands, with no other islands in sight, and this is where they just *happened* to get shipwrecked.

On top of all the other weirdness, it certainly seemed as though this was somehow supposed to happen.

This line of thought continued as she drank a bit more water. *A forest that was big enough for them to have wood to chop up for fires, but not so big that they could get lost.*

What other conveniences are there? she wondered.

She realized she'd been gone longer than she wanted to be, so she had a few more mouthfuls of water, got to her feet, and headed back toward the container.

While she walked, she also realized, though, that there would be no big animals—like the boar she'd imagined earlier—living on the island. There would probably just be whatever fish they could catch in the ocean, plus the bodies of her fellow travellers.

She let out a dark little laugh as she arrived back at the container, thinking, *Oh, yes, what a lifesaver Pigscouge's compass is going to be.*

"Where were you?" Fishstench said when Goatbaler pulled herself back up and into the container. "And who said you could take Gigglesheen's hatchet?"

Everyone was awake now, and most of them looked terrified. Some were feigning grief at the loss of their five container-mates.

Goatbaler wasn't a big fan of sexist language—at least not while others were actively listening—but she couldn't help thinking, *Sweet Jesus, what a bunch of pussies.*

Cowherder, in particular, was inconsolable, his wife, Gristlespoon, being one of the deceased. Him she could understand, but the rest of them? Jesus. They'd barely known each other.

"Well, the rest of you were asleep, and I didn't want to wake you up. Would you rather I just roused everyone from their slumber to announce I was leaving? What point would that have served, exactly?"

Fishstench looked displeased by her answer, but no one else was pushing Goatbaler on this logic. Most of Fishstench's bravado was performance-based, so if no one was egging him on, like a proper bully he was happy to let the issue slide.

If there was no social credit to be earned—just like on Facebook or Twitter—what was the point in sticking your neck out?

Surprised that he didn't push her on her answer, Goatbaler, switched subjects. "Anyway," she said, "I found fresh water on the other side of the island."

No one said anything.

"Ummmmmmmm, you're welcome," she said, her voice dripping with sarcasm.

Still no acknowledgement. Mudherder just mumbled "Boom" quietly under his breath. It was like a nervous tick he physically couldn't stop.

"Boom, indeed," Goatbaler said, and rolled her eyes. This annoyed Mudherder, but he didn't want to be seen as assailing "her truth" in some way, so he let it go.

"Wait, you made it all the way to the other side of the island?" asked Twirlfluff.

"*All the way* isn't that far, Twirlfluff. The whole island is about a quarter of a square kilometre, give or take. Not big."

"Is that not big?" Twirlfluff replied. "It sounds fuckin' big."

"Go out and look for yourself," Goatbaler said.

"We'll *all* go out," Fishstench said, seeking to regain control of the group once again. "And," he added as people started getting to their feet, nursing their aches, pains, and bruises, "we'll find somewhere to bury our fallen comrades."

Several people objected to this, but the most vehement was Goatbaler. She argued that she'd seen the size of the island, had seen that there were no other islands in sight. There were no boats on the water. There wouldn't be any wildlife to kill and eat. "And it isn't like we were gifted a fucking fishing pole and tackle box. We'll die on this island in a matter of two weeks, tops, if we don't *eat* our 'fallen comrades'."

Someone gasped. Someone else gasped right after, thinking they should virtue signal their astonishment.

Goatbaler made a farting noise with her mouth. "You

can all be as outraged as you like, but this is about survival now, not about decorum, or proper burials, or anything else. It's about having enough food for eighteen people to eat. I know it's a horrible thought, but we need to be real about this. We're not pushing this container off the sand anytime soon to float around aimlessly in the ocean. Can we agree on that?"

Some people nodded. Others looked around the container to see who was nodding, and did the social-cred mental calculation about whose side they wanted to be *seen* to be on, then either nodded or didn't based on that math. (Whose side they were *actually* on was another matter altogether).

Trying to out-woke your fellow social justice warriors must be exhausting work. To be successful, you had to forever play both sides of a constantly shifting set of goal posts, always ready to jump onto the "right" side of whatever issue sprang up.

Our island castaways hadn't quite realized that their audience was gone, and that they were really only performing for each other now.

Since the consensus was still far from clear, Fishstench decided to continue to argue. When the point was settled (hopefully in his favour), he wanted the narrative to be that he'd *clearly* been on the side of burying the dead. It wouldn't help for him to have been seen waffling.

"Have some respect, Goatbaler," he began. "These are our *friends* who have died."

"Well, some of them were," somebody muttered.

Fishstench ignored the heckle. "And the idea that we're just going to *eat* them is disgusting and, I would argue, entirely premature. Why are you advocating for this reprehensible course of action?"

"Look," Goatbaler answered. "Can we go outside and get some fucking air? It's hot as balls in here."

"Do you have to use that sexualized language?" Cangbritches said. She was running on auto-pilot at this point. "I understand that, like, we're stranded and everything, right? But patriarchy is patriarchy, and you're only enabling—"

Goatbaler simply stopped listening and walked toward the container's hole. She jumped down into the water. She poked her head back in, said, "Follow me out here if you want, or don't. I don't give a fuck right now."

Everyone exchanged looks of confusion.

The woke handbook hadn't prepared them— Goatbaler included—for the eventuality that they'd be stuck on an island, faced with the choice of whether to bury or eat their colleagues. No social media to appeal to in an effort to gauge the temperature of their echo chamber's opinions. Nowhere to look to cobble together their "truth" on the matter of cannibalism.

Would the *New York Times* have had something to say on the matter? Would NPR have had something to add?

Why had no one published *Island Survival for the Insufferably Woke*?

Once they'd all gathered outside, they argued a little more about the pros and cons of burying the deceased, then they put it to a vote. It was close, but the motion to bury them won the day: 10 for; 8 against.

"Okay, so exactly how are you geniuses gonna bury these five people?" Goatbaler asked. "How will you dig a hole six feet deep? The hatchet? The hunting knife? The fucking multi-tool?"

Everyone looked around, muttering and shrugging.

"Ah," Goatbaler said. "A well-thought-through plan."

"Look," Fishstench said, "we'll take them into the forest and just heap soil on top of them, maybe some big leaves if we can find any."

Enthusiastic nods of agreement rippled through the group.

"And just hope the stench doesn't assail us, I guess," Goatbaler replied, but with much less gusto. It was clear people wanted to bury the dead, give them proper respect —which Goatbaler would actually have been absolutely in favour of, had said dead people not been their only current source of sustenance.

"And besides," Fishstench added, "you were outvoted, Goatbaler. The motion has passed. I suggest we get to it."

Goatbaler glared at Fishstench, but said nothing. She tried to think of something cutting to say, but her energy for the argument was flagging. Resigned, she just shook her head, then finally said, "Fine, but I'm not helping you."

"Suit yourself," Fishstench replied. Moving back into the container, he said over his shoulder to the others: "Come on, folks, let's bury our friends."

The sun baked seventeen of the survivors—those carrying their five fallen comrades. Well, to be clear, it baked them all, but only ten were carrying the five corpses—one on each end, under the shoulders and cupping the feet. Well, okay if we're gonna get granular, eight people were carrying shoulders and feet, but in Stinkberry's case, the last few greasy strings of skin and muscle tore free when they started dragging him, and his head came off. So one person had Stinkberry's head tucked under an arm. Gigglesheen got stuck with said head, and had an appropriately disgusted look on his face.

Goatbaler watched them slog their way first through the sand, then reaching firmer ground when the trees started coming into play. While she watched, her anger boiled. She turned toward the water, as if looking for some sign of fish, but again knowing deep-down in her gut that there would more than likely be none.

Around and around in her head while she watched them struggle with the weight of the carcasses: *They're burying our food, they're burying our food, they're burying our fucking food!*

Barely aware her feet were moving, she literally followed in the group's footsteps.

Most of their backs are to me. They won't see me coming. I have to do this. I have to do this. For all our survival, not just my own.

Her hands on auto-pilot, she reached for the hatchet and the knife in her waistband. Fifty steps away from the last person in line.

Forty steps.

She dropped the hatchet in the sand—it would only slow her down.

Thirty steps.

Twenty.

Ten.

The knife gleamed in the blinding island sunshine.

Five.

Zero.

None of those carrying the bodies' feet had turned to look behind them; none of those carrying under the shoulders had looked up from their burden.

Goatbaler's natural swing was about lung-height. She likely didn't know it, but this fact certainly came in handy for dispatching her victims in a timely manner.

Chickenpicker was the first to get it. Goatbaler jabbed him in the back as hard as she could, once on each side, left and right. He cried out once, and dropped.

Goatbaler moved quickly to the next back she saw: Mudherder's. Stab-stab. Same treatment. He yelled out "BOOM!" one last time, then fell over backward, blood already pooling in his lungs.

Gigglesheen was next. By this time, Goatbaler was entering her stride, so she landed three blows. *Pop-pop-pop!* Goatbaler imagined she could actually hear the lungs popping this time. Gigglesheen fell forward atop Stinkberry's headless corpse. Twitched a few times, groaned once, then was still.

Someone screamed as reality finally began to sink in. That said, they continued carrying their cargo for a few seconds longer—just long enough for Goatbaler to claim her fourth victim.

Cowherder, still cupping Gristlespoon's feet in his hands, tears streaming down his face, turned around just before Goatbaler struck. His face was expressionless, resigned to his fate, lost in his grief. He may have said, "Thank you," just before she struck the first of her two blows: one to her customary lung-location, the second to his neck, and he curled inward after the first blow doubled him up. Blood shot up in a jet-spray, which fanned out as it arced into the air, his body drifting to the sand in seeming slow-motion.

By this time, people had clued in to what was happening, and had dropped the bodies they were carrying. Nearly everyone scattered, ran into the forest.

Their fearless leader, Scooter Fishstench, vamoosed like the rest.

Husband-and-wife team Sheepchaser and Barn-greaser, however, decided to be heroes. They yelled at Goatbaler to put the knife down. The took up positions, one on either side, arms extended, palms open in a supplicant position to try to show her they were no threat.

But Goatbaler's blood was up. She shrieked, blood streaking her face from arterial spray. It was *High Tension*, but set on an island. Goatbaler moved back and forth between the two would-be heroes, slashing at their hands.

The first to make a move was Barngreaser. He was tall. He was the man. He would subdue her—even at the cost of social media later calling him a misogynist for undercutting Goatbaler's righteous feminine rage.

While Goatbaler slashed the knife toward Sheepchaser, Barngreaser lunged, tackled Goatbaler, falling upon her like a tree in the forest falling on a deer.

He succeeded in tackling her, but Goatbaler pulled the knife up to her chest just before the pair fell to the bloody sand.

The knife lodged in his chest, drove straight through his heart.

Barngreaser choked once, twice. His eyes went wide. Then his head dropped onto the sand about half a foot above Goatbaler's head.

Sheepchaser bellowed her rage and grief to the uncaring sky above. She Darth Vader'd the shit outta the scene, dropping to her knees, and screaming, "Noooooooooooooooooooooooo!!"

Goatbaler was still insane with bloodlust. She grunted, puffed, and pushed with all her might, trying to get the behemoth Barngreaser off of her. Finally, she pushed hard enough, and his body fell to the side, enough for her to wiggle out from under him.

She rose to her feet, panting, soaked in blood. She strode over to Sheepchaser where she still knelt in the sand, wailing to the heavens.

"Shut," Goatbaler said, slashing Sheepchaser's throat quickly. A torrent of blood issued from the wound, drenching her chest and stomach in moments.

"The fuck," another strike, this one to Sheepchaser's left eye, puncturing it.

"Up," she finished, and jabbed the other eye out.

Sheepchaser stopped caterwauling. Fell forward into the sand.

Goatbaler breathed heavily through her nose, her eyes wide open, unblinking, staring down at the corpse at her feet. She turned around, saw the other five bodies.

She stood like that for what seemed like a millennium, until her breathing evened out. The red she'd seen smearing her vision while she rampaged slowly receded.

Her mind cleared enough to speak. The words when they came seemed spoken by another person—some murderous demon who'd taken over her body for the last two minutes, then relinquished it as its bidding had been done.

She yelled out so that everyone—no matter where they'd hidden—would hear: "Hunting knife! Multi-tool! Duct tape! Hatchet! Lighter! We'll need these items to cut up and eat these bodies!"

No one said anything for a few moments. Waves lapped the shore. Birds squawked overhead.

Then someone yelled out from the forest: "What's the duct tape for?"

Goatbaler closed her eyes for a moment, pushed down her annoyance. "To tie the wood together that we use to make a spit!"

Another moment of fresh air slipping in off the ocean. The breeze ruffled Goatbaler's hair.

Then the questioner from the forest said merely, "Oh."

Goatbaler wiped the blood-soaked knife on her shirt, turned around, headed back toward the shipping container, bending and picking up the hatchet on the way.

Having murdered six people, Goatbaler became the new de facto leader of the container castaways. Fishstench did not object; he had seen Goatbaler in action, and was just as terrified of her as the others.

If Goatbaler's diary is to be believed, Fishstench didn't speak another word until his own untimely—and decidedly gruesome—demise.

But I'm getting ahead of myself.

Crocodile tears were shed for the fallen, then the castaways got down to the business of carving up the eleven corpses.

Before they had definitively settled on beginning this terrible work, Goatbaler had satisfied their queries about fish. As she'd suspected, there were none to be found. All twelve castaways fanned out across the island—it was so small, it didn't take long—and they all returned with the same news that they hadn't seen a single living fish, nor any other ocean-dwelling creature, for that matter. The only other animals seemed to be birds, mocking them from above. A couple of worn-out container-mates halfheartedly threw rocks up at them, but missed by miles.

Hunters and gatherers, this crew of spoiled westerners certainly was not.

Goatbaler appointed those with the strongest stomachs to take the first carving shift. Only after they grew exhausted would the next shift come online. They decided to dismember and carve the carcasses inside the shipping container—so they themselves were out of the blazing heat, but also so that their future meals would be, too.

Goatbaler sent a handful of people out into the forest with the hatchet to chop whatever wood they could to build a fire, as well as for duct-taping together to create the spit she'd mentioned earlier.

While two shifts alternated back and forth carving with the hunting knife (only the second crew falling victim to vomiting several times)—and the others hatcheted the forest for wood—Goatbaler washed herself in the ocean. Most of the blood came off her skin easily, but her clothes would remain tinged red until she could properly take them off and beat them against rocks.

She thought the murders had gone as well as they could have, all things considered, but something kept niggling at the back of her mind.

If their kidnapping had all been somehow (supernaturally?) orchestrated, as she couldn't help thinking it was—the convenient fresh-water pond; the lack of fish where there should be plenty, forcing them to kill each other for food; this particular manifest of container castaways, etc.—shouldn't there be some way to keep the bodies cool? Like, the shipping container could have been refrigerated—though it could easily have been damaged when it crashed up on the sea stacks. Besides, how would it have continued running on the island? Goatbaler didn't know enough about refrigeration units to speculate. . . . Hmm, what else?

Then it hit her: *A cave? Maybe there's an underground cave on the island? Somewhere cool enough to at least keep the bodies chilled long enough to eat? It wouldn't have to be for too long—twelve people eating eleven bodies. . . . And hell, I can just murder some more when I get hungry.*

She laughed darkly to herself while she rinsed blood out of her hair.

Re-entering the shipping container, Goatbaler gagged a little at the sight and smell that greeted her. Body parts lay strewn about everywhere. The walls were splashed a dark red that she would see in her dreams most nights from that point onward.

What have I done? she thought, before her mind snapped closed on this line of inquiry. *That way lies only hopelessness and despair. Have to focus on the situation at hand.*

"I have a hunch about something. Maybe a place to keep things cold. Gather all of—" she waved a hand in the general direction of the impromptu slaughterhouse "—*this* together in one spot, then wash the container as best you can. I'll be back as soon as possible."

Hatchet and knife visible in her waistband—she didn't tuck her T-shirt over the weapons because she wanted people to see that she still had them—she dropped out of the container again, splashing into the water below.

She headed to the closest edge of the forest, then began walking its outer edge methodically, looking for the imagined cave.

Since it was so small, it didn't take long to do a full circle of the island. As she did so, for the next pass she moved inward a little, tried not to cover any ground she'd already been over. She could have asked someone for help to get the search done quicker, but she didn't—*couldn't*—trust anyone at this point. They could all just easily fall upon her and kill her, eleven to one, but they were still in shock at what she'd done, so she reasoned she was safe for now. But the shock would wear off soon enough, and she'd need to be prepared for that eventuality.

About half an hour later—roughly her fourth pass inward and around the tree line—she spotted a dark little hole that looked somehow unnatural. She bent down, poked at it, moved fallen leaves and branches away from its opening. It widened as she did so.

Bingo, she thought. *I fucking knew it. Whoever's responsible for this doesn't want us to starve to death; they just want us to cannibalize each other.*

Another dark laugh popped out of her mouth like a grunt she was barely aware of.

Once she'd cleared a bit more out of the way, she saw the full scope of the hole—it wasn't just a hole in the ground; it actually rose up beyond the earth, giving way to the side of a small hill, like a bunker.

She continued clearing more forest leavings out of the way. That's when she reached it, and she could barely believe what she was seeing.

It didn't only resemble a bunker, it *was* a bunker. Hidden into the side of this small hill.

It even had a door.

She tried the door's metal handle.

The door was not locked. Of course it wasn't.

She cleared some more branches out of the way of the door's path, then pulled it completely open.

She stepped inside. The room was about 12 x 12 feet. It was cool. Not cold, but definitely cool.

Cooler than it should be, though, even closed off from the heat, and shielded from the sun by the trees as it is, she thought.

Then something else occurred to her.

I wonder . . .

She walked back outside, leaving the door open, just on the off chance it might lock if she closed it. She traced the outline of the small hill, found herself around back of it—and sure enough, just as she thought but dared not hope for, there was a generator.

She pulled on the engine's cord. Once, twice. Three times. On the fourth try, she put her back into it, and it roared to life.

She walked back around to the front, inside the bunker again, and felt along the back wall until she found the hole where the cold air was pumping in.

When she left the bunker, she closed the door firmly behind her.

Crazy, she thought. *This is madness.*

At this point in Goatbaler's diary, events take on a sort of montage quality. Things apparently moved quickly once the bunker was discovered, so she had little time to make diary entries: The job of hauling the carcasses over to the bunker. Cleaning the bodies. Chopping wood from the forest to fashion their spit. Settling on the best way to build said spit. Arguing over the best/healthiest way to cook "the meat."

It surprised even Goatbaler herself that she seemed to have no particular qualms about murdering people with the *intent* of eating them but, as a social media performance-vegan, the thought of *actually* putting the meat in her mouth was the thing that brought her close to puking.

They decided not to build huts or any other structures in the forest, but would continue using the shipping container as shelter. (It seemed stable, propped against the sea stack and driven deeply into the sand as it was.) Twenty-three was a fairly tight squeeze with regard to personal space in there, but between the sea stack's storm intervention and Goatbaler's killing spree, they were nearly down to half of that now. Twelve would sleep pretty comfortably.

During their excursions looking for decent wood to use, they came across some edible berries (which helped reduce the monotony of their forced all-meat diet), as well as a poorly hidden cache of gas cans—fifteen in total—that ensured they wouldn't run out of refrigeration any time soon.

As they went about their business, they would occasionally congratulate each other in solemn, fake-earnest tones for their bravery in deciding to cannibalize their dead friends.

One notable entry in Goatbaler's diary as they came to the end of what I think of as the "island-set-up montage" is a single entry on an otherwise clean page that simply reads: "We are as a train on a track, barrelling toward a destination we can know nothing about. The engineer has cut the brakes, and only he knows where the track ends."

With their daily routines firmly in place—chop wood; pick berries; fetch water from the pond using the canteens; prepare food; cook food; eat food; occasionally wash their clothes and themselves in the ocean; sleep; repeat—the initial uplifting mood of feeling somehow *taken care of* began to wear off. Societal cracks began to show. More arguments broke out over mundane things. A couple of near fistfights between the men. Name-calling and general shitting-on-your-heart behaviour from the women. Several "safe spaces" were designated around the island for when people were perceived to have acted inappropriately, so that the offended party had somewhere to, I don't know . . . recuperate?

No doubt it was a stressful situation for everyone, but they were proud of themselves that they hadn't just given up, committed suicide. Hope still presided over their little ragtag crew of survivors.

Goatbaler's diary entries start picking up again in more detail about six days after the bunker discovery. She relates an incident that one would think was a delusion caused by their strange new diet, or perhaps sun stroke, but there is evidence that it actually happened.

And it would change the course of their remaining time on the island.

On the seventh day, just as the sun was beginning to set, Goatbaler was roused as she drifted off under a tree not far from the beach, near the shipping container.

She opened her eyes slowly, dreamily. The others were setting about that night's dinner, or nodding like her under nearby trees, their work shifts over for the time being.

She heard the weedy little voice before she saw the person who owned it. Horsegrazer hadn't said much since they'd arrived on the island, so it was surprising when Goatbaler heard this very voice bellowing at everyone in a commanding tone.

She looked up, and thought perhaps the twilight was

playing tricks on her.

Was he wearing a robe? Where the fuck did he get a robe?

Horsegrazer had told everyone he was "going wandering" two days earlier, but Goatbaler assumed he'd been back to eat, drink, etc. But maybe he'd just been on the other side of the tiny island losing his mind.

A small cliff rose up from the shore about forty feet above the sea stack and the container. This is where Horsegrazer stood.

With what appeared to be two stone tablets in his hands.

The bellowing had brought the others to the beach, too, and everyone gathered near Goatbaler—as scared of her as they were, they knew she was the fiercest one there, and would at least protect them against whatever might come their way during the next few moments.

Now that she'd shaken off the sleep cobwebs, Goatbaler got to her feet, and watched incredulously as the scene unfolded.

Horsegrazer's long hair made him look kinda like Jesus, or Moses, or someone biblical, anyway. This coupled with the robe and the tablets, and you've got a very strange and alarming scenario shaping up.

It was under these conditions that Horsegrazer now spoke:

"Cannibals!" he shouted, perhaps forgetting that he'd eaten Soylent Green, just like the rest of them. Maybe he'd eaten a raw brain, and was now suffering from Kuru?

Then: "You have sinned a great sin in the sight of The God of Woke!"

Everyone exchanged confused glances. Most of them thought of themselves as pretty woke, so what was this bullshit?

"You are not worthy," Horsegrazer continued, "to receive these Ten Woke Commandments!"

"Where did he get those?" Jellypuff asked quietly.

"And that robe? Where's that from?" Flitternose added.

Goatbaler turned around and said, "I know, right?"

Horsegrazer looked to be struggling with the tablets' weight now, shifting them uncomfortably from side to side, trying to get a better grip. He presumably didn't just set them down at his feet because he had a Big Moment planned.

"Oh, shit," Gumphook said, snapping his fingers. "He's doing Chuck Heston in *The Ten Commandments*. Dunno where he got the get-up, but those are definitely some of Chuck's lines from the film."

Everyone was familiar with the film, of course, but only Gumphook seemed to know the lines off by heart.

"Hell, I'll play along," he said excitedly—anything to alleviate further boredom. "I might not get it exactly right, but let's see what I can remember."

He cleared his throat, and stood with a fist over his heart.

"You take too much upon yourself," Gumphook shouted up at Horsegrazer. "We will not live by your commandments—we're free!"

"There is no freedom without the law!" intoned Horsegrazer.

"Whose law, Horsegrazer, yours?"

A few castaways had settled in for the show, sitting cross-legged, munching absentmindedly on a meaty forearm or calf.

"Did you carve those tablets," Gumphook continued, really digging deep into the role now, "to become a prince over us!?"

"Who is on the Lord of Woke's side, let him come to me!" Horsegrazer said, sweeping his arm over the group of castaways.

"He's actually doing a pretty good job," Pigscouge whispered to Dirtplanter.

There was a pained expression on Horsegrazer's face, though, and it was clear he didn't have the strength to hold the tablets aloft for the whole scene, so he gently set them down, and continued.

Unlike in the film at this point, no one started panicking and running around. Horsegrazer looked a little deflated by this fact.

Gumphook continued the scene happily.

"He showed you no land flowing with milk and honey! I showed you a God of Gold! Come with me! Follow me!"

Gumphook went so far as to turn to the other survivors, spreading his arms wide as if to take them all in.

Horsegrazer pointed at Gumphook, and swept his eyes over the others. "Blasphemers!" he said. "Idolaters!"

So many exclamation points.

"For this you shall drink bitter waters. The God of Woke has set before you this day His laws of life. And good. And death. And evil."

With great effort, Horsegrazer bent down and picked up the tablets, stacked them together as Heston did in the film, and concluded this scene with a mighty flourish:

"Those who will not live by the law . . . shall die by the law!"

He threw the tablets as far as he could—which was maybe two feet, tops. They made it to the edge of the section of cliff he stood on, landed with a soft thud, and just kind of slid unimpressively down the rest of the way to land in the sand.

Dirtplanter clapped. Snowmint followed suit, just in case anyone ever accused her of not supporting her fellow castaways. As a proper moral coward, she wanted to be on the right side of whatever situation occurred.

Gumphook bowed.

Horsegrazer looked winded.

Everyone went back to their food prep, napping, etc.

The tablets sat in the sand the rest of the night. Only in the morning did someone besides Horsegrazer bother to read them.

THE TEN WOKE COMMANDMENTS

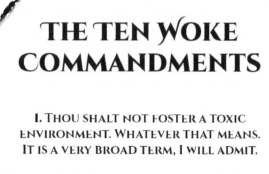

1. THOU SHALT NOT FOSTER A TOXIC ENVIRONMENT. WHATEVER THAT MEANS. IT IS A VERY BROAD TERM, I WILL ADMIT.

2. THOU SHALT NOT BULLY. BUT IT IS TOTALLY FINE TO BULLY PEOPLE YOU PERCEIVE AS **YOUR** BULLIES—TO THE BRINK OF SUICIDE, IF NECESSARY. EYE FOR AN EYE AND ALL THAT.

3. THOU SHALT NOT TAKE THE NAME OF THE LORD THY WOKE GOD IN VAIN. ALSO, NO PATRIARCHY. AGAIN, FAIRLY VAGUE, BUT YOU KNOW WHAT I MEAN.

4. REMEMBER BLACK SABBATH DAY, TO KEEP IT HOLY. NOTHING AFTER OZZY. WELL, MAYBE SOME DIO, BUT DON'T GO NUTS. OH, AND BE ON THE LOOKOUT FOR MICROAGGRESSIONS. THEY'RE TINY—BARELY PERCEPTIBLE, IN FACT, UNLESS YOU'RE STRAINING TO FIND THEM—BUT THEY'RE **EXACTLY THE SAME** AS MAJOR OFFENCES. DON'T ASK WHY; I WORK IN MYSTERIOUS WAYS.

5. HONOUR THY FATHER, MOTHER, AND ALL DESIGNATED SAFE SPACES. THERE IS NO NEED TO GROW UP AND DEAL WITH THE WORLD AS IT PRESENTS ITSELF.

6. Thou shalt not murder. Unless it's someone you think might be racist, misogynistic, homophobic, transphobic, or generally not as woke as you. Don't worry about due process—just murder them where they stand. If you don't wanna do the time, open an anonymous Twitter account and accuse them of horrible shit till they hang themselves.

7. Thou shalt not commit body-shaming or slut-shaming. Most other types of shaming are okay—especially woke-shaming, since it furthers the narrative. Oh, and definitely the public shaming of your enemies. Dox those fuckers if you can get away with it.

8. Thou shalt not steal. Nothing special about this one. Just don't rob other people of their valuables. Even if you want to, like, **suuuper**-bad.

9. Thou shalt not appropriate thy neighbour's culture. Other cultures' beautiful art, dancing, clothing, food, and music is off-limits to you. You do not get to enjoy them in any form. Be happy with what your own people did, and stop trying to enjoy your fellow human's creativity.

10. Thou shalt not covet wokeness. If you feel you are not woke enough, you probably aren't. However, good news! Intolerance is learned, so just hang out with your more-woke friends longer, and you'll be more intolerant of diverse viewpoints before you know it!

"Wow," said Gumphook. "These are very informative."

Snowmint had joined Gumphook to investigate Horsegrazer's discovery that following morning. They each brushed the sand off of one tablet and took turns reading them aloud to each other. As they did, their voices began to take on a tone of awe and wonder. By the time they reached the end of each tablet's divine contents, their eyes were wide as saucers.

"OMG," said Gumphook. "We have to tell the others. These are brilliant."

"Yes," said Snowmint. "They articulate everything I've always felt in my heart, but have been unable to put so succinctly into words!"

Each cradling one tablet to their chest, they reverently walked back to the shipping container. They banged on the sides of it to wake everyone else up. "Come out, come out!" they shouted. "These tablets are amazing! You must come out now!"

While the other castaways groaned and shifted inside the container, slowly rousing themselves to see what all the hullabaloo was about, Snowmint and Gumphook propped up each tablet in the sand on the shore, displaying them as best they could in the morning light.

Once everyone had gathered on the shore, Snowmint and Gumphook instinctively joined hands, and began to speak.

"Behold!" they said in unison. Then Snowmint swept her free hand over the two tablets, and let Gumphook deliver the Good Word.

"Lay thine eyes upon these tablets, fellow castaways, and know that the words inscribed thereupon are good and true!"

Everyone dropped their eyes to the words carved into the tablets. As they read, their eyes went wide, just as Gumphook's and Snowmint's had. The one exception was Jellypuff, who eyed the tablets suspiciously.

"Come forward, Horsegrazer!" Gumphook said, his voice full of emotion. A single tear fell from his left eye as he spoke. "Come bask in the holiness of the Word you have delivered from out of the darkness of the woods!"

Horsegrazer wiped sleep from his eyes, and walked toward Snowmint and Gumphook. When he was near Snowmint, she reached out and took his hand.

"You guys didn't much care about this last night," Horsegrazer said.

"We didn't know what lay engraved upon the surfaces. Please forgive us!" said Gumphook, who then bent to one knee and bowed his head.

Not particularly liking the religious-cult direction this was headed, Jellypuff—easily the least woke remaining on the island—said, "Where did you find those, anyway? And the robe, too?"

Horsegrazer shrugged, and said, "I was just bored out of my mind, so I went for a wander around the island. Got a bit turned around, stayed out longer than I'd anticipated. Anyway, on the far side of the island—" he motioned vaguely behind him "—there was a little bush that looked a bit strange, sort of misshapen, unnatural, so I went over and kicked it out of curiosity. The tablets were hidden inside. The robe was underneath them."

"Amazing," Snowmint said.

"Meant to be," said Gumphook.

"Was the bush burning?" asked Hoghauler in a rare speaking role.

No one laughed.

Like Fishstench, Hoghauler had been terrified into silence for fear of stepping wrong, and being destroyed for it. I mean, people were being fucking murdered here, and he was no idiot.

"Look, let's just take it easy," said Jellypuff. "Let's try to look at this rationally, shall we?"

Of course, now that the others had read the Good Word, no one wanted to hear a dissenting voice—least of all one touting *reason* and all its systemic oppression. The dictates on those tablets spoke to them all so directly, so powerfully, that no common-sense rationale was going to penetrate their minds at this point.

"Shut your mouth, Jellypuff," someone said angrily.

"Yeah, shut it, dummy," another voice chimed in. "Who are you to question the divine inscriptions on these tablets?"

"Jesus Christ, I'm just trying to say we should approach this skeptically, considering how weird this whole situation has been ever since we inexplicably found ourselves in the shipping container. Also, a lot of those 'commandments' or whatever they are—they're pretty crazy, don't you think? Like, maybe going a little too far?"

Goatbaler wanted to agree with Jellypuff, but she looked around and saw the fervour in people's eyes, and felt her command slipping away. People had allowed her to be in charge because they viewed her as unhinged, ready to murder at the drop of a hat. But once religious doctrines begin to take hold in a person's mind—and they believe wholeheartedly in them—fear of physical danger becomes greatly lessened.

So Goatbaler kept her mouth shut.

But Jellypuff was stubborn, and decided to dig in on this point. Naturally, Flitternose—being Jellypuff's wife—was onboard, too.

"Take for instance," Jellypuff said, "Point number nine. It says—"

"Um, excuse me," Cangbritches interrupted. "It's a *Commandment*, not a *point*."

Jellypuff ignored her, and carried on: "It says not to 'appropriate' other people's cultures. But isn't it just as much my 'fault' that I'm white as it is someone else's that they're black, or brown, or whatever? None of us should be punished for what we simply *are* by happenstance of DNA."

Blank stares all around.

Jellypuff continued, undeterred: "To attain true equality, isn't the goal to do *away* with a hyper-focus on racial- and gender-based identity? If people are defined by the colour of their skin or what's between their legs—and how they use it—how can humanity ever move beyond those genetically random markers?"

The blank stares had turned to frowns now. Genuine anger was boiling up. People clenched their fists, breathed heavily through their noses.

Goatbaler felt an uncomfortable shift in the air. She instinctively stepped back, decreasing her proximity to Jellypuff and Flitternose.

Jellypuff, perhaps feeling he'd already gone too far, audibly gulped, but finished his thoughts with these last few sentences: "So . . . shouldn't we all be judged solely on our individual personalities and actions—on 'the content of our character,' as MLK put it? If we can all share freely in each other's cultures, wouldn't that lead to a better understanding of our fellow humans in general? Surely, dialogue in search of common ground, not the things that separate us, is a better way to attain equality—even when that dialogue makes us uncomfortable, or causes us to question our own viewpoints. How can the socially progressive way forward be to make *further* distinctions between people, rather than *fewer*?"

For a moment, Jellypuff's words hung in the charged air.

Then, as one—barring Goatbaler, who had moved back from the crowd—they descended upon him. Kicking, punching, screaming, pulling as hard as they could at whatever part of him was available to their hands.

Flitternose yelled, "Not my Moontouch! You leave my Moontouch alone!"

Half the crowd immediately leaped off Jellypuff, and tackled Flitternose.

They literally tore them both limb from limb. Blood splashed the two Commandment tablets. One of them got knocked over when someone launched Jellypuff's head over their shoulder. It smacked against the tablet with a dull thud.

Goatbaler did nothing to stop it. She just walked slowly backward, keeping her eyes on the frenzy.

I've lost control of them, she thought as she snuck away. *There's no way their fear of me can stack up against those Commandments. And since I didn't join in on taking down Jellypuff and Flitternose, they'll all be against me.*

Now she was conflicted.

Should I go back and act like I was there from the start? Hope they believe that lie? No, too risky. Even though their blood is up right now, and their memories of who was there and who wasn't could be called into question, the truth will likely out when they've calmed down. They'll know I wasn't involved from the start, and they'll call my faith in the Commandments into question.

She turned around, and broke into a full run, heading for the forest.

She was now a pariah.

She knew she could never go back.

Goatbaler watched from a distance, hiding in the forest, as her remaining fellow castaways dragged the destroyed corpses from the beach (after washing the bodies in the ocean, of course). They were being taken to the bunker for prep and storage.

Thinking of the future, she'd have to work out a way to sneak into the bunker when no one was looking—likely at night—to steal food. She'd have to go to the opposite end of the island, and build her own fire—fuck, they had the lighter! *I'll have to figure out how to get a fire going old-school*, she thought. *By rubbing two sticks together or whatever. Ugh. Like shit isn't difficult enough as it is.*

Goatbaler walked toward the other side of the island. Suddenly, a great sweeping sense of relief made her so light-headed she nearly fell over: *I still have the knife and hatchet in my waistband.* She stopped walking, moved her hands to feel them. *How will they chop their wood and carve their food now, huh? They need me.*

Then a very dark thought occurred to her: *If they can't find me, they'll never get these tools. They'll starve to death. Or at least be reduced to eating raw human flesh. And they'll die from that, anyway, won't they?*

She didn't know the particulars of raw human meat consumption in this regard, but the idea of them being so desperate that they would eat raw flesh made her smile.

She held onto the hatchet and hunting knife so tightly, by the time she reached the edge of the treeline, her knuckles were white.

In another diary-montage, Goatbaler relates how she chopped down some trees for wood to create a make-shift shanty-type dwelling that probably wouldn't protect her much from the elements, but was the best she could do. During that first night alone, she went on a brief midnight raid to swipe some duct-tape to lash the wood together.

She wondered how much food she should take that night, eventually deciding that—since the distance was so short, and she still had the most powerful weapons—she would only take what she needed for two, maybe three days. If anyone caught her in the act, she was confident she could take them down.

And hey, that's just more food in the end, isn't it? she thought, and chuckled.

Through trial and error on her second day alone, she eventually discovered the best way to start a fire using just wood. She made a spit on which to cook her food, but it was a much smaller version of the one at the main camp. There was only one of her to feed, so why waste the energy creating more than required?

What she didn't know, of course, is that nearly everyone would be dead within the next three days, anyway, so these preparations hardly mattered.

Goatbaler's remaining diary entries—as they pertain to what was said between the remaining castaways—should be taken with a grain of salt due to the fact that she had to hide behind rocks and trees at the treeline, essentially straining to eavesdrop on their conversations. She was apparently able to make out a decent portion of what was said, but she admits to filling in the blanks with her own interpretations of events.

It's also around this point in her diary that she begins to realize that, barring outside intervention—they'd written several SOS messages in the sand; tried reflecting the sun using the signal mirror; turning the flashlight on and off at night, making sad attempts at Morse code; and even blowing the plastic whistle—only one person was going to survive on this island. Eventually, the rest would either starve or be killed for food, depending what level of civility people managed to maintain.

And that final person would then, themselves, starve.

She didn't dwell too much on it for fear of falling into depression, but it's clear that she realized this was the likely outcome.

She slept fitfully those first two nights apart from her previous tribe. Then, on the third day, with tempers beginning to flare, food starting to run low, the Commandments being the only social glue holding them together, and only a multi-tool with which to defend themselves, things began to collapse quickly.

Three would die that day.

Four the following day.

Then two the final day.

Leaving only one alive.

On the first of those three final days, Goatbaler had picked a spot near the cliff where Horsegrazer had made his ridiculous presentation, hid herself near some bushes. She was fairly close to the container in this spot, and the echo was strong in there, so she was able to pick out a good deal of what was being said.

The trouble began early in the morning.

Raised voices drifted out of the container, latched onto a puff of ocean breeze, and carried swiftly to Goatbaler's waiting ears.

". . . is *so* a micro-aggression!"

"Is *not!*"

"Is *so!*"

Someone else tried to calm the two arguers, but neither party was having it.

"Stay out of it, Horsegrazer!" they both shouted in unison.

Horsegrazer shut his mouth. His role as the island's Moses hadn't quite settled into his skin yet, so he was still taking the occasional order.

Cangbritches defended her position: "You said I should —and I quote—'Eat more than a fucking bird'!"

"I did not say 'fucking,' and you *should* eat more than a bird!" Pigscouge replied. "You're a human! So I'm saying you should eat like a human!"

"Exactly," Cangbritches said, bony hands on her non-existent hips. "And that's a body-shaming micro-aggression!"

"Oh, puh-lease! Take it as a compliment. You'd blow away in a strong breeze!"

Several people gasped.

If there had been a handful of fence-sitters on the "eat like a bird" comment, all doubt was now removed: Pigscouge was absolutely body-shaming Cangbritches. Something that was clearly in violation of Woke Commandment #7. Not to mention #4. Two clear transgressions had taken place.

Goatbaler perked her ears in the direction of the container to see how they would handle the situation—their first real test of the Commandments.

Horsegrazer looked toward Fishstench in the hope that maybe he would reassert himself as the group's leader, but he just stared straight ahead, still unwilling to speak.

Horsegrazer realized he may have to assume the role of leader. At least for the time being. No one else was stepping up, and he *was*, after all, the one who'd found the Commandments, and brought them to the group. Why *shouldn't* he be their leader? Their moral conscience, if you will.

Confidence began to burgeon inside his chest, and he decided to try it on for size. "Okay, okay, regardless of intent, clearly Cangbritches was hurt by your words, Pigscouge. Maybe if you—"

Cangbritches saw where Horsegrazer was headed with this, and so she cut him off immediately, shouting at

Pigscouge, "No! No apologies! You don't *get* to apologize!"

Everyone just looked at their feet.

"Well, I wasn't going to, anyway, you skinny little bitch!" Pigscouge said, and threw the group's compass at her head, narrowly missing it.

"Alright, okay, settle down, please, and we'll sort this out democratically." Horsegrazer was enjoying this feeling of power he suddenly had. He'd never really had any in his pre-island life, and it was addicting. He was beginning to see why people enjoyed it.

Surprisingly, all eyes were now on him. Even though several castaways really didn't like him, they had to admit that he *was* the deliverer of the Commandments, and that could never be taken away from him.

The privilege of power grew inside him, puffed his ego.

He held his head high, pushed his chest out, and spoke— unsure of where the words were coming from, but delivering them with distinct authority: "We will vote on the matter. Raise your hand if you believe that at least one Commandment has been violated."

Cangbritches immediately threw her hand in the air.

Five more people put their hands up.

The remaining two voters saw this, and thrust their own hands into the air as fast—but as naturally—as they could. No one wanted to be seen dissenting from the group. Intellectual honesty had always been unwelcome on the island, but with rigid Commandments now in play, the pressure to bend to the group's will was even stronger.

"There it is, then," Horsegrazer said, "It's unanimous. You have been judged by your peers to have violated at least one Commandment."

Everybody continued staring at him.

"So what's the punishment?" Snowmint finally asked, voicing what was undoubtedly on everyone's mind.

"Well, since an apology clearly isn't acceptable," Horsegrazer said, just kind of winging it, "and public humiliation isn't possible, considering our socially isolated situation, I suppose . . . death?"

Everyone nodded, and happily agreed.

Everyone except Pigscouge.

Who immediately made a run for it.

Pigscouge didn't get far, of course; she didn't even get out of the container.

Dirtplanter tripped her as she ran past, sending her sprawling. She landed facedown, then rolled herself onto her back, and began begging for her life.

Twirlfluff kicked her in the ribs, a look of disgust on her face. "Shut yer fuckin' mouth. You did this to yerself."

Cangbritches saw her opportunity—a fallen enemy, lying on her back, being kicked when she was down—and pounced. She straddled Pigscouge where she'd fallen, and wrapped her hands around Pigscouge's throat, began choking her. Twirlfluff held her arms so she couldn't fight back. Snowmint sat on her legs so she couldn't kick free.

Pigscouge gasped, her tongue lolling out of her mouth. Cangbritches squeezed tighter and tighter, using all her strength to choke the life out of the bigger woman.

Cangbritches' face was filled with not only rage, but

the unmistakable appearance of glee.

Pigscouge struggled for another minute or so, then her prone form went limp.

Silently, the castaways carried her body out of the container, and brought it to the bunker for preparation.

"It's a shame it had to come to that," said Dirtplanter solemnly while she gnawed on Jellypuff's blackened calf.

Dinner was served, and the group was filled with an appetite-inspiring righteousness.

Twirlfluff, chewing on one of Flitternose's ribs, licked her lips, and said, "Yeah, not much we coulda done about that. She knew the rules."

Even though the crucial details of those rules—and their punishment—had been made up on the spot.

She took another bite, then added, "Fuck, I wish we had some barbecue sauce."

Their source of meat was getting low. They had the rest of Jellypuff and Flitternose, and now all of Pigscouge, but being leaderless the past couple of days, they hadn't been rationing with any sort of plan in mind, and they'd gone through a lot more meat than they should have.

Goatbaler expressed to her diary that she thought people were subconsciously fatigued at the idea of continuing in this fashion, and were throwing caution to the wind.

Near the "dinner table"—basically just a bunch of large leaves and bits of flat(ish) wood surrounding their fire pit—Gumphook was struggling with the multi-tool's knife, trying to hack through various bits of Pigscouge.

"You know," he said, "if we had that hunting knife or hatchet back, this would be a lot easier. Why don't we fan out and try to find Goatbaler, get our tools back?"

There were a few grumbles, but no one seemed excited about the idea. Goatbaler had shown herself to be formidable with those weapons, and no one seemed keen to walk straight into death's arms just yet—even with the Commandments on their side.

"I wonder how she's doing," Dirtplanter said, but no one took up that thread, either. As far as the group was concerned, she was dead to them. She hadn't joined in on the mobbing and killing of Jellypuff and Flitternose, so there was no way back for her.

They knew it, and they knew that *she* knew it.

"Our laws," said Gumphook absentmindedly while he sliced a length of muscle from Pigscouge's carcass, "are merciless but necessary."

Even if people disagreed, no one could voice their disagreement. Diversity of thought would not be tolerated.

They just nodded and chewed in silence.

"I'm heading off to a safe space, you guys," said Snowmint. "I'm feeling a little overwhelmed and anxious right now. I'll be back soon, though."

Everyone wished her well, half-heartedly asked if there was anything they could do to help, then went back to their meals.

Snowmint stood up, walked toward the closest designated safe space about fifty feet away.

Goatbaler followed her. She knew she could get quite close because, once inside, Snowmint wouldn't be able to see much except through the small safe space's opening.

There were six safe spaces on the island, all of which were strictly off-limits to anyone but the user. They were basically just leafy branches arranged to form a very small hut-type structure, in which a person could sit inside cross-legged and tune out the island for a little while.

The castaways had agreed on a universal "occupied" signal so it would be obvious when a certain safe space was being used: If the biggest branch on top of the little hut was placed with its leafy end angled *toward* the entry hole, the hut was occupied; if the biggest branch was placed with its leafy end angled *away* from the hole, it was available.

You can see how this might cause some problems due to confusion, but it was the best system they could come up with, so they stuck with it.

Snowmint angled the biggest branch toward the entry hole, then entered the safe space, sat cross-legged, closed her eyes, breathed deeply, and—Goatbaler imagined— tried to clear her mind of the negative energy of the day. She probably felt like there might have been a bit of bullying directed her way, and maybe a microaggression or two, but for as long as Goatbaler had known her, she had never wanted to be one of *those* women—the kind who overreact. Snowmint considered herself very level-headed in this regard. She was confident that she never overreacted because she was on such guard for it, but that others often did. She felt sorry for them. How awful to be that sensitive—not that it was their fault, of course. They were just living their truth, the same as everyone else.

Several minutes passed while Snowmint breathed deeply. Then Goatbaler heard a rustling close by. She tucked herself deeper into the foliage in which she hid.

Definite footsteps now, getting closer, crunching twigs, leaves.

Then a scream.

"What the fuck!" shouted Snowmint, crawling out from her safe-space hole. She stood up, brushed herself off, and began berating someone.

From what she could tell, it looked to Goatbaler that Dirtplanter had mistakenly tried crawling into the safe space with Snowmint.

"Oh, I'm so sorry," Dirtplanter said, sounding fairly calm—seemingly unaware of the seriousness of her transgression. "I didn't know someone was in there. The leafy part of the biggest branch was angled toward the hole, so I thought it was empty."

"When the leafy part is angled toward the hole it means the safe space is *occupied!*"

"Oh," said Dirtplanter. "I thought it was the other way around. I'll just go find another safe space. Especially now that I'm feeling attacked."

"Oh, *you're* feeling attacked, are you? Well, how do you think *I* feel!? Being intruded on in a *supposed* safe space —and not only that, but being *touched without my permission*, as well!"

"But I only brushed against your leg by accident as I was trying to get in. I didn't mean—"

"Your intentions don't matter, Dirtplanter; you know that as well as I do—as well as we *all* do. You can't feign ignorance of that now. Just face up to what you've done!"

Dirtplanter was no fool; she knew she was doomed. The rest of the group would see things Snowmint's way— and would be swayed by her cries of victimhood. Nothing Dirtplanter could say or do would matter now.

She felt tears welling, knowing this would be the end of her life.

"Nothing else to say for yourself?" Snowmint gloated, arms crossed, knowing the group would side with her.

Dirtplanter hung her head, turned around, and started walking back toward the container.

Snowmint followed, a grim little grin touching the edges of her mouth.

It was an unspoken truth that the victim of any Commandment violation would be the transgressor's murderer.

And so it was in Dirtplanter's case.

As expected, once the case was brought to the remaining castaways, it was an 8–0 unanimous call— Commandments #5 (dishonouring safe spaces) and #1 (fostering a toxic environment) were deemed to have been violated. This time, three people weren't quite sure how to vote, so they waited until they saw which way the wind was blowing, and quickly joined the winning team, their own morals and scruples be damned.

If there'd been a Retweet or Like option for the decision, they'd have done it in a heartbeat.

Even though, intellectually, she knew it was coming, Dirtplanter was still shocked to see the unanimous declaration that she should die for what she did. The blood drained from her face. Her legs gave out from under her, and she plopped down into the sand.

She began to weep quietly.

No one batted an eyelash.

Snowmint grinned, asked to be handed the emergency flashlight, and moved in.

Without another word, she beat Dirtplanter to death with the flashlight, destroying it in the process.

No one seemed bothered by the destruction of the emergency flashlight; they all knew they weren't getting off this island.

A few hours later, night fell, and the remaining seven castaways (barring Goatbaler, who had unintentionally taken on the role of the island's Virgil) were seated around a fire pit. Horsegrazer had taken to constantly wearing the robe he'd found in the bushes, under the Commandments. He never took it off now—not even to wash it. He simply dunked himself in the ocean every once in a while, fully robed. And when he sat at the edge of the fire pit, he always sat in the lotus position.

Everyone wanted to roll their eyes, but Horsegrazer was sharp, and was always darting his eyes around to see if anyone was taking the piss. He wanted them to so he could exercise his newfound power, command that the offending eye-roller be destroyed for a microaggression.

The mood was subdued. The usual ravenous tearing into of meat was not occurring tonight. People nibbled unenthusiastically at the various calves, forearms, ribs, and flanks of their former friends and colleagues.

Twirlfluff decided to try to lighten the mood by gathering up the two dildos, the ball gag, and the Fleshlight (they kept all the survival gear that had been issued to the dead in a pile, in case any of it were needed).

"Look at these fuckin' things," she said as she returned to the group, waving around the two dildos in her hands. She sat down cross-legged, dropped the dildos between her legs, picked up the ball gag, strapped it on around her head, and popped the red ball in her mouth. She tried speaking around it, but the words were unintelligible, which made her start laughing. And once she started, she couldn't stop. She picked up one of the dildos, inserted it into the Fleshlight, and mimicked sexual intercourse.

In, out.

In, out.

More uncontrollable laughter. Tears now streamed from her eyes. No one knew what she was saying, but she appeared to be making up some sexual scenario, and acting it out with the available props.

Surely, she had to know this wasn't going to fly in this crowd. But it seemed like maybe a screw had come loose, and this scene before the group was her unravelling.

In, out.

In, out.

Laughter. Snorting.

No one else laughed. There were now just expressions of pity and horror around the fire pit as they watched this mental breakdown unfold.

Slowly—very, very slowly—people's heads turned toward Horsegrazer. Beseeching a course of action, he knew.

Their eyes seemed to be saying, *What shall we do with this laughing hyena? This disgusting jackal in the guise of a woman?*

Horsegrazer let the moment wash over him: These six fellow travellers looking to *him* as their leader. Looking for *his* guidance. He had wanted this sort of power for as long as he could remember, and now—finally—he had it.

"If ever," Horsegrazer said in a slow, even tone, eyes still closed, "there were an example of the violation of the First Commandment. This—" he motioned toward Twirlfluff, who was now trying to jam both dildos into the Fleshlight, with little success "—this is it."

Twirlfluff paid him no mind. Drool dribbled down and around the ball gag, pooling in her lap. Her tears of laughter suddenly changed to tears of sorrow. She was having trouble breathing around the ball gag, but she made no effort to remove it from her head.

Goatbaler, using the moon for light, and watching wide-eyed from the shadows, scribbled madly in her diary as the scene continued.

After another full minute of this bizarre behaviour, Twirlfluff began screaming behind the ball gag—a muffled, tortured sound, as described by Goatbaler, that "haunted me for the duration of my remaining days on the island."

Finally, Twirlfluff threw the two dildos at Horsegrazer, hitting him in the chest. When she began fisting the Fleshlight—a mad, dazed look in her eyes, pig-like grunts issuing from her gagged mouth—that was all people could handle. Horsegrazer sensed the shift in the group, and knew it was time to act.

Horsegrazer stood quickly, asked Gumphook for his help. Gumphook stood, ready to help in whatever way he was asked.

"Take one end, and help me lift" is all Horsegrazer said, as if he were speaking of a table.

Horsegrazer did as he was directed.

They lifted Twirlfluff from the ground by her armpits and feet, and carried her toward the ocean.

They drowned her there in the glow of the moon.

"A strange sacrifice to the God of Woke," said Horsegrazer quietly, gently removing the ball gag from Twirlfluff's mouth once she'd taken her last breath.

Gumphook nodded solemnly.

Together, they pushed her body toward the horizon. The tide took it graciously, and offered silence in return.

The next day, the remaining survivors wanted to question Horsegrazer about his chosen method of Twirlfluff's "removal," but—after much hushed discussion about how best to approach such a delicate topic, given Horsegrazer's seemingly divine providence—they decided against inquiring further. They didn't want to question his methods or motives, lest they be charged with violating Commandment #10, coveting wokeness.

Their main query, had they the moral fortitude to go through with questioning Horsegrazer, would have been: *Why would you waste meat when you know we're low on food?*

In the end, no one said a word for fear of being labelled a disbeliever. A dissenter from Horsegrazer's truth.

And Horsegrazer himself did not comment on the episode again. That window to dialogue was closed.

The castaways were now down to the remnants of

Jellypuff and Flitternose, plus Dirtplanter's full corpse. Not a lot of food for six people—not to mention Goatbaler the thief making matters worse, sneaking in and stealing from her former group every now and again.

The necessity of further killings had unintentionally been baked into their survival plan. So it was really just a matter of who and why.

It was only cognitive dissonance that kept them from attacking each other in a frenzy. They were holding both modes of thought in their heads at once: strictly adhering to the Commandments and their ensuing punishments, while also fully aware that only one person would come out of this alive.

But no one spoke openly about their dire situation. Maybe they thought the God of Woke would simply provide. Or that the God of Woke only gave one as much as one could handle—the same ridiculous happy crappy attributed to the Christian God.

It was mid-afternoon on another brutally scorching day—the convenient fresh-water pond was beginning to dry up, having had no rain in a while. But again, no one spoke of this development.

Fishstench—now freed of any obligation to speak, or try to contribute in any meaningful way—had gone for a hike up the side of the island's one small cliff, above the shipping container's final resting place against the sea stack. The scene of the weird *Ten Commandments* reenactment.

He had looked sad when he'd embarked on his little

trip, taking only a canteen of water and the group's little signal/hygiene mirror. Gumphook had asked why he was bothering with the mirror; they'd tried everything to get rescued, but no boats had ever been seen on the horizon, and no planes had ever flown overhead.

Fishstench just shrugged his shoulders, effectively communicating, *Why the hell not? What do we have to lose?*

Tough to argue with that.

Goatbaler watched with interest as Fishstench—a seeming husk of his formerly blustery, overly confident self—made the fairly short trip up the scree of the cliff-face, picking his way through bushes and bramble to get to the top.

So, as with Horsegrazer's epic Commandments, another such scene was about to play out—only this one would be as if from a silent film.

Once at the top of the cliff, Fishstench raised the little mirror and gazed at himself in it for a long time. Tears streamed down his cheeks, and the castaways all gathered on the beach to see what would happen.

They could see his shoulders shaking as he sobbed while he stared at his reflection. But rather than turn the mirror to reflect the sun, ostensibly to get some would-be rescuer's attention, he bent down to a nearby rock, and cracked the mirror against it, just hard enough to break it into two pieces.

He then set the two pieces aside for a moment while he wrote something in the dirt.

Standing back up, he took one final breath, then drove one shard of mirror into each eye, jabbing them deep enough (as one investigator noted later on) to slice into his brain.

He toppled forward off the cliff, his body slamming with a loud, sonorous *thud* onto the top of the shipping container.

A bird circled overhead. Cried once. Twice.

Then only the sound of the waves accompanied Hoghauler and Snowmint as they moved toward the container—on Horsegrazer's order—to retrieve Fishstench's broken body.

This put everyone in a slightly better mood as their rations had suddenly doubled.

Even though they'd all seen Fishstench write something with his finger in the soil—essentially a dead man's final words—no one had any interest in venturing up to see what they were.

No one, save for Goatbaler, that is, who—skirting around the island, attaining the top of the cliff from the back way where no one could see her ascent—read Fishstench's last words, and copied them down in her diary:

"I have violated Commandment #2. In my time on this earth, I have bullied friends, enemies, and everyone in between. I see now that—especially as a white man—I am toxic, and every bit a part of the problem as those I bullied. I offer my life as a sacrifice to the God of Woke, whom no doubt I have failed despite my best efforts to honour through my spearheading of public humiliations. Godspeed, my friends. Please enjoy my broken (but no doubt tasty) carcass. I suspect I am fairly well-marbled."

Hoghauler wasn't in the best of shape, having been a smoker and overweight most of his life, so he cut a somewhat pitiful figure huffing and puffing his way up onto the roof. It had taken three people to push his butt up there after stepping into Gumphook's interlaced fingers for the initial boost.

He finally scrambled up, though, then spent five full minutes on his back recovering from the ordeal.

Snowmint was in better shape, so she didn't have much problem. As she clambered up onto the roof, leaning forward to pull herself over the lip, she glanced up and saw Hoghauler watching her.

She met his eyes, then frowned, but didn't say anything until she was securely on the roof. She then waited until he dragged himself to his feet before saying, "Were you looking down my top?"

Hoghauler blushed immediately, blood rushing to his face. "What? No, I— I—" he stammered.

"When I was leaning forward to pull myself up here a moment ago, I saw you looking. You were looking down my top. Don't try to deny it. I saw where your eyes went."

More stammering, but he didn't deny it. How could he? She had *told* him not to deny it, so if he tried to now, that would be seen as a microaggression. It would also be seen by the others as not believing the victim. He knew, too, that he couldn't apologize—regardless of whether he'd done it or not. Again, microaggression.

The only option left open to him was to cast his eyes down. Maybe if he just waited sheepishly like that, she would have mercy on him.

"Anyway," she said after what seemed like an eternity, her voice taking on a slightly calmer tone. "Let's get

Fishstench off of here. But keep your eyes on the job, got it?"

Hoghauler said nothing, just kept his eyes averted, and reached down to pick Fishstench's mangled body up under the armpits.

Snowmint leaned over—her eyes glued to Hoghauler's face, lest his eyes even inadvertently flick anywhere in the vicinity of her chest—and grabbed Fishstench's feet.

They shuffled over a little with the body, moving it closer to the edge of the shipping container, where they planned to toss it down to the beach.

Hoghauler kept his eyes low, but as they struggled with the weight of the corpse, he couldn't help himself, and knew as soon as the words were out of his mouth that he'd signed his own death warrant. He said, "If you hold his legs more under the calves rather than just holding his feet, the weight will distribute a little more evenly, and it will be easier on my end, too."

Snowmint stopped in her tracks.

Hoghauler knew what came next. He flushed again, and just waited for the words to come out of her mouth.

"Are you seriously," Snowmint said, dropping her end of the carcass, "mansplaining to me how to carry a dead body?"

Hoghauler dropped his end of the corpse. "No! No, no, I wasn't. I swear. I was just trying to make it an easier job for both of us. Honestly."

He knew his explanation would hold no water, but words were all he had as defence. It's all anyone has in defence against false accusations. Fat lot of good it does in such a situation, but he was desperate. He didn't want people thinking he was that kind of person. And he didn't want to die.

Snowmint glanced over her shoulder.

Everyone knew the drill. Time to vote.

Hoghauler had no way to prove he hadn't looked down her top. He had no way to prove that he wasn't mansplaining. You cannot, after all, prove a negative. He knew he was finished.

Cangbritches' hand shot up enthusiastically. She was nearly dancing on the spot at the thought of seeing another man murdered. She'd had a field day when the "KillAllMen" hashtag had been making the rounds on social media. After all, one less man equals one less patriarch to keep women down.

Gumphook made a point of not meeting Hoghauler's desperate gaze while still raising his hand slowly.

It was already two out of three, so Horsegrazer didn't need to participate, but he did anyway, because he wanted it known to the group (such as it was) that he was, indeed, on the side of the angels.

Snowmint smiled broadly, turned back to Fishstench's corpse, yanked a shard of mirror out of his left eye with a grunt, then moved toward Hoghauler with purpose.

"Whoa, whoa, hang on, please, let me—!"

Snowmint swung the shard in a wide arc. It sliced Hoghauler's belly open. She swung again the opposite way. Another slice—this one even deeper than the first.

Hoghauler looked amazed and baffled at this development. His hands moved to his stomach to try to hold his guts in, but a coil slipped through his fingers. He saw this, shit himself, and passed out where he stood, falling like a sack of potatoes.

Snowmint kicked his stinking body off the lip of the

container in disgust. It fell facedown in shallow water with a splash.

"Pigfuck," she said, her hand now bleeding from the deep cut the shard had made as she swung it.

She walked back to where Fishstench's body lay. She kicked that dead sack of meat off the container, as well, and said, "You, too."

Snowmint then walked to the opposite end of the shipping container, where the water beneath her was deeper. She jumped off. The salt in the ocean stung her wounded hand, but she barely felt it, so full was she with the spirit of woke righteousness.

She waded back onto the beach, high-fived Cangbritches (with her good hand) as she passed, and headed to the main camp area to get the first aid kit.

Seeing evidence of Snowmint's ferocity, Goatbaler was glad she'd chosen to leave the group when she did. She was good with her hatchet and hunting knife, but she wasn't sure she could have matched Snowmint's sheer driving bloodlust.

It must be said, too, that given the tone of her diary entries from this point forward, the desire for retribution on this scale of intensity wasn't within Goatbaler anymore. She looked back on her murder spree, and almost felt as though someone else had killed those people. Could she have appeared like Snowmint just did? That unhinged? That hellbent on the destruction of another human life?

She shuddered at the thought.

She realized she'd been holding her breath for most of Hoghauler's murder, so that when she started breathing normally again, she became light-headed.

She closed her diary, and walked quietly back to her part of the island.

Four left, she thought.

Well, four left. And me.

"Hahaha! 'Trash with eyes.' That's great," said Cangbritches.

Later that evening, half of Dirtplanter turning on the spit, the smoke from the fire drifting up and into the moonless night, the remaining four castaways were actually getting along pretty well. In the outside world, they had gotten along decently, and they mostly liked each other. Through all the murder and horror on the island, a new bond had undoubtedly been established.

They were the final four—in it together till the end. True survivors of the unfair hand they'd been dealt. Victims of the highest order.

"That *is* pretty great," said Gumphook.

"Riiiiiiiight?" Cangbritches replied.

There was still no rain on the horizon, and the pond was definitely drying up. There was still enough to fill all the canteens for a few more days, but beyond that . . .

"Trash with eyes" had been how they'd referred to Twirlfluff—and several other of their dead compatriots—behind their backs.

Horsegrazer looked on somewhat disapprovingly, since this gossip *could* be interpreted as a microaggression, or even bullying, but now that the person being attacked was dead, did it still count? There was no Commandment to cover bullying the deceased—

and Horsegrazer was in a good mood tonight—so he let it slide.

"Dirtplanter's actually tastier than I thought she'd be," Gumphook said.

"Don't be so insensitive," Snowmint replied, but with insouciance. A smile played about the corners of her lips.

Gumphook looked up sharply at first, but then— seeing that Snowmint wasn't actually offended—laughed nervously, and bit a little harder into one of Dirtplanter's ribs than he'd intended, nearly chipping a tooth.

The good mood, of course, would not persist, but the final four certainly did enjoy their last meal together.

There had been so many arguments and murders over the past few days, Goatbaler admitted she'd had trouble keeping the details about them straight in her diary, but she was doing her best.

"Well, at least I'm not the town bike!" Cangbritches suddenly shouted in Snowmint's face. The argument had broken out not long after dinner when they'd been clearing up. Snowmint had made an offhand comment about how she'd lost track of Cangbritches' "various sexual shenanigans."

Snowmint had chuckled after her comment, and had clearly said it in a non-judgmental, sex-positive, playful manner. Just another example of the not-woke-enough failing to properly read a room. Naturally, Cangbritches took massive offence, citing the slut-shaming portion of Commandment #7, and they were off to the races.

Even under the best of circumstances, there was no

room for missteps, but in Snowmint's current milieu, it was literally a life or death miscue. All of which she *had* to have known, of course, so one is forced to wonder how much the murder and cannibalism of their friends and colleagues had taken a mental toll—even on the wokest amongst them.

Gumphook knew to stay out of it, else be seen as a white knight, a microaggressor, patriarchal, or any number of other minefield-adjacent concepts.

Horsegrazer, too, knew to stay quiet—less out of fear, though, and more out of curiosity to see where things went.

Snowmint slapped Cangbritches across the face.

Cangbritches, probably about a head shorter than Snowmint, reeled from the open-palm strike, nearly falling over backwards. She turned her head back slowly toward Snowmint, and said, crisply and clearly: "You fucking butch cunt."

Gumphook's mouth gaped open.

Horsegrazer's eyes went wide, and his eyebrows retreated nearly to the back of his skull in surprise.

Cangbritches screamed, and leaped up on Snowmint, tearing at her hair, dragging her nails across Snowmint's face. (This gender-stereotypical fighting style was an embarrassment to them both.) Blood immediately welled up from deep wounds on Snowmint's face and neck.

Snowmint bellowed her rage, and managed to disengage the smaller woman from her upper body, pushing her off with both hands and onto the ground at her feet. She kicked out once, hitting Cangbritches in the stomach. Cangbritches gasped for breath, fell backward into the dirt.

Nearby, the fire crackled; the smell of an overcooked Dirtplanter filling the smoky air.

Snowmint tentatively brought a hand to her face and neck, felt the slickness there, brought it back in front of her where she could see it. Saw the red.

And lost her shit entirely.

She lunged at Cangbritches, windmilled her fists as fast as she could. She caught Cangbritches twice solidly in the face, but the remaining blows didn't land.

But it was enough to bring the fight to an end—for both of them.

In her blind rage, Snowmint didn't see the direction in which she was forcing Cangbritches to backpedal, and she wound up pushing her right into the fire. The spit with Dirtplanter's blackening half-body toppled to one side, and Cangbritches fell in backwards, her hair lighting up instantly in a halo-esque burst.

She screamed, and was about to try rolling out of the fire pit when—still enraged, arms insanely pinwheeling—Snowmint tripped on the edge of the pit, and fell directly on top of Cangbritches, knocking her own head against a particularly large log on the edge of the fire in the process.

Cangbritches was pinned to the ground.

Inside the fire pit.

She tried to push the now-unconscious Snowmint off of her, but she was too small and weak. (And too on-fire, it must also be said.)

Snowmint's hair and face started to blacken.

Cangbritches screamed until her lungs filled with smoke, and she could no longer create sound. She continued thrashing beneath Snowmint, whose entire back and head were now engulfed.

Snowmint never regained consciousness. Perhaps in an uncharacteristic moment of mercy, the God of Woke spared her that pain.

Not so for Cangbritches; she felt every lick of flame, every lung-scorching inhalation until the flames fully consumed her, too.

Nothing alive moved in the fire pit now.

But the flames continued to dance.

The next day, Horsegrazer and Gumphook shaved off as much burnt flesh from the carcasses as they could, but some pieces were still like biting into pure charcoal. There wasn't a lot to be salvaged, so they decided to just eat what they could of these two bodies, and save the remaining "good ones" for future meals.

Gumphook took another bite, and thought but didn't dare say, *Tastes like bitches.* He grinned at this, and Horsegrazer caught the smile out of the corner of his eye while he chewed some gristle. "Something funny?" He said this with no affect, so Gumphook wasn't quite sure how to respond.

Even with the island inhabitants being decimated— now down to just the two of them, and Goatbaler, wherever the hell she was hiding—Gumphook wanted to be on the right side of either possible equation. If by some wild happenstance, they were suddenly rescued, Gumphook still wanted to be on Horsegrazer's good side, since he was the one to which the God of Woke had shown the Commandments. If he turned on the robed weirdo now, and they *were* rescued, who would the world side with and believe—the guy in the robe with the Jesus hair carrying the tablets of sacred Commandments, or regular ol' nothing-out-of-the-ordinary him?

No one wants to get publicly humiliated by the messiah.

With this in mind, Gumphook answered Horsegrazer's query with, "Oh, nothing, just happy to have a full belly."

As the day wore on—the two men going about their own business, occasionally coming together for meals—Goatbaler observed Horsegrazer acting a little strange toward Gumphook. Somehow . . . suspicious of him.

Furtive glances when Gumphook wasn't looking. Longer-than-normal eye contact when he *was* looking. It was subtle, but she'd been watching these people for days and days now, and she'd subconsciously picked up on a lot of their normal behaviour, and this wasn't it for Horsegrazer.

Eventually—as twilight began to fall, and the winds picked up, slapping waves against the sea stacks and shore —Horsegrazer approached Gumphook, held his head back, puffed his chest out and said, "You've never liked me, have you?"

Gumphook, cornered—it was true; he'd always loathed Horsegrazer—looked away, began sputtering nervously, hoping that whatever came out of his mouth would assuage Horsegrazer. "No, it's not that, certainly not, it's just that—"

Horsegrazer held up a hand. Gumphook stopped blathering.

"It's okay, I understand. I'm an acquired taste. And I'm painfully socially awkward, I know."

Gumphook said nothing, just waited.

"The thing is . . ." Horsegrazer said, and let the words hang dramatically in the air.

Goatbaler was watching in the woods, as usual, while she waited to see who would kill whom—for surely, that's how this had to go.

While she watched this exchange, though, straining to hear what they were saying, she noticed a distinct change in Horsegrazer's body language. He seemed somehow much more dangerous, like something was bubbling just under the surface, and some recent event—or perceived event—had brought this new *swagger* to the forefront.

That wasn't quite the right word, but mere confidence didn't cut it; it was more than that.

Goatbaler moved her hand to her waistband, curled her fingers around the hatchet handle there.

"The thing is . . ." Horsegrazer said again, but this time finished his thought. ". . . I think you're coveting my power. I think you want what I have. You want to be what I *am*, what I've *become*. The God of Woke speaks through me now. I am His vessel, and you want to *be* me: the moral conscience of our group."

He seemed unaware that two people do not constitute a "group."

"I see it in the way you stare at me," Horsegrazer continued. "I catch you in moments when you think I'm not looking, but I am. And what I see in your eyes is pure covetous envy."

"No, absolutely not. I—"

Again, Horsegrazer held up a hand to stop Gumphook's protestations.

"It's okay. It's not your fault. But it *is* a violation of Commandment #10, and you *will* need to be punished for it." He pulled the multi-tool out of one of his robe pockets, and stepped toward Gumphook.

Goatbaler pulled the hatchet out of her waistband, cocked her arm back, stood up. She did some quick emotional math, and realized she'd much rather be stuck on the island with Gumphook than with Horsegrazer, so if the latter started getting the upper hand on the former, she knew in whose back she would attempt to land the hatchet.

Gumphook backed away from Horsegrazer, keeping his eyes pinned to the multi-tool. Horsegrazer used his free hand to pop out the bloodied knife extension. It was all they'd had to carve up a bunch of those bodies, so it was caked in blood, and looked very dull. No doubt it could still go through someone's guts, though.

Gumphook continued backing away, hands extended open-palmed. Words failed him now, but he kept shaking his head from side to side. When he felt his feet and legs splashing into the ocean at the shore, there was a faint *thwack* sound, and Horsegrazer stopped moving. His eyes opened ever so slightly wider, and he looked very confused for a moment, before falling forward with a hatchet in his back.

Gumphook glanced down in shock at the body lying at his feet. Waves gently lapped against Horsegrazer's head, swishing his long hair around.

Gumphook then looked back up to where Horsegrazer had been advancing on him, and saw Goatbaler standing there, hunting knife in hand, ready to finish Horsegrazer off, if necessary.

"Holy fucking shit, thank you," Gumphook whispered, then said it again louder, so Goatbaler could hear him.

For a long moment, Goatbaler didn't respond, then she simply nodded. "Is he dead?" she asked.

Gumphook looked down. Horsegrazer didn't seem to be moving, but it was a bit tough to tell due to the motion of the water around his body and head. Gumphook looked back up at Goatbaler, and shrugged.

She began marching toward the pair on the shore of the ocean, hand still wrapped around the knife. Her eyes drifted down as she walked, just enough to notice something out of place sticking half in, half out of the sand.

Pigscouge's chopsticks. *Oh, that's right; she got the compass* and *the chopsticks. Thought she was special. Ha.*

Goatbaler bent down, picked up the chopsticks. Miraculously, neither was broken, even though they'd been on the beach, likely being stepped on and kicked around, for who knows how long.

She grinned, then put the knife back in her waistband.

"Take out the hatchet, and roll him over," she said to Gumphook when she reached him.

Gumphook did as he was told. The hatchet came out with a tiny *pock* sound, then Gumphook used his foot to roll Horsegrazer over.

When he was fully on his back, Horsegrazer coughed once, violently. Blood speckled his face from the expulsion.

Gumphook yelped, startled, and scurried behind

Goatbaler—even though he was currently the one with the most dangerous weapon. Realizing he didn't want the responsibility, he handed the hatchet back to Goatbaler, who tucked it into her waistband with the knife.

Horsegrazer opened his eyes with great effort. They tracked around in his head until they found Goatbaler standing above him. He opened his mouth to say something—probably some ridiculous woke/religious bit of bullshit.

But the world would never know, because without another word, Goatbaler straddled him, and jammed the chopsticks into his eyes as hard as she could.

She felt them travel through the softness of his eyeballs, then his brain, then splintering on the back of his skull.

That night, the moon was full and beautiful. It gleamed off the ocean, shimmering, sparkling.

Goatbaler and Gumphook sat together near the fire pit, on the same side, nearly touching knees, as though they subconsciously wanted each other's emotional comfort.

The nights were getting colder than when they'd first arrived—the only true indicator of a broader passage of time.

As they warmed their hands by the flames, Gumphook was the first to break the comfortable silence.

"So," he said, grinning a bit. "We've got enough food for a week or two, I think, if we ration it better than we've been doing for these past few days when things began to—" he searched for the right word "—really break down, I guess you'd say."

Goatbaler returned his grin, but an outside observer would probably have said hers was a little sadder than his. He was like a dog who was happy to just go along with whatever made things easiest. Goatbaler liked to think she was a bit more complex than that.

Even so, they were both exhausted, and were having trouble keeping their eyes open. Especially with the warmth of the fire, and the gorgeous view of the reflected moon on the ocean waves. It almost seemed for a brief moment that they were on a legitimate vacation together— their respective significant others not only not on the island with them, but not even *existing*.

For that brief moment, Goatbaler thought she was another person entirely. Someone experiencing a fleeting pang of conscience, perhaps.

It was in that moment—when she explicitly felt that she was *not* herself—Goatbaler turned to Gumphook and said, "Aleksandër was a good friend to us. What we all did to him was a shitty fucking thing to do."

Gumphook at first flinched at the mention of my name, but he composed himself, seemed to gather his thoughts, and replied, "Well, I think we did what we felt was right at the time, and what we thought was best for our—"

In one swift movement, Goatbaler reached into her waistband, pulled out the hunting knife, leaned forward quickly, and drove the blade into Gumphook's neck, embedding it to the hilt, then yanking it out and leaning away from him so he couldn't grab her, had he the presence of mind or automatic reflex to do so.

Blood splashed her face as the artery she'd hit pumped with his heartbeat. She jabbed the knife twice into the other side of his neck.

Gumphook gurgled once, fell sideways. Gasped for air a couple of times. Then was silent.

The moon lit Goatbaler's path like an accomplice as she dragged Gumphook's body to the refrigeration bunker.

Goatbaler lived off the meat in the bunker for the next two weeks, rationing herself just enough each day to barely get by without passing out.

The canteens continued getting filled with the remaining water in the pond, but soon enough that ran out, too.

Rain had not fallen in weeks, and there was no sign on the horizon of any coming.

This is probably just as Aleksandër wanted it, she thought. Certainly there was no doubt in her mind—as her diary entries made clear—that I was somehow behind the whole thing.

That sense of victimhood she'd learned from social media—being the biggest victim: the most marginalized, the most downtrodden, the most overlooked, the most historically unseen, the most historically unheard, to keep racking up those friends, those likes, those hearts, those retweets, those shares—was coming to the forefront now.

As the food ran out over those final two weeks, the water soon to follow, and the sun continuing to beat down on the island even more oppressively than usual—with the lessons of social media swirling in her protein-deficient brain—she knew what she had to do.

If she were going to die alone on this wretched island—and she hadn't had real reason to hope otherwise for weeks—she would need to leave one final tweet.

A posthumous tweet in the sand for all to see.

And even now—when she didn't believe anyone would rescue her before she starved to death—she still believed her sand tweet would be found intact.

She began composing it in her diary.

At first, she decided to keep it old-school Twitter, with just 140 characters, really challenging herself to make it brilliant, but she quickly realized she'd need the full 280 to really make it pop.

While her body feasted on its remaining fat stores, and just as it started to move onto stripping her muscles and shutting down her organs, she used a stick to write the final tweet in the sand—not so close to the water that the tide would erase it, but not so close to the treeline that it would be hard to spot by a passing aircraft.

She drew a box around the tweet, and even traced a little heart in the sand in case someone wanted to "like" it.

The sand-tweet read:

DEAR WORLD,

ALEKSANDËR EATON IS RESPONSIBLE FOR OUR DEATHS. NONE OF US WHO DIED HERE DESERVED THIS FATE. SOMEHOW, IT IS HIS REVENGE ON US FOR WHAT WE DID TO HIM. WE

CANCELLED HIM, SO NOW HE HAS, QUITE LITERALLY, CANCELLED US. BUT WHAT WE DID WAS FOR ALL OF YOU.

Goatbaler wasn't entirely sure what she meant by the last line, but she knew it would be viewed by social media as being profound, selfless—something a true martyr would say as she starved to death.

She dropped the stick once she'd finished writing the massive tweet in the sand. Then, using the last of her remaining strength, she made her way toward the cliff.

On the way, she kicked over the Ten Woke Commandments tablets where they still jutted out of the sand where they'd been propped an eternity ago. It wasn't that she didn't believe in them—she did—but she had begun to question her methods for bringing about that kind of change.

She only really wrote about these doubts on one page of her diary, but it was a crystal clear window into her thinking on the matter.

On the very last page of her diary, she wrote in big block letters:

OUR LIES AND HALF-TRUTHS TOLD FROM GLASS HOUSES HAVE FOLLOWED US TO OUR GRAVES. WE ARE NOT SO PERFECT.

When she reached the top of the cliff, she collapsed flat on her back, severely winded and in a good deal of internal pain, and looked straight up into the bluest sky her eyes had ever known.

She expired like that quietly—cardiac arrest—staring at the sun, a quizzical look on her face, as though this giant ball of gas 93 million miles away were a riddle that she was just on the verge of figuring out.

Or perhaps, less poetically, as if she were about to sneeze.

According to the official investigation notes, not more than an hour after Goatbaler took her final breath, a plane flew by overhead, and saw the writing in the sand.

PART III:

AFTER THE ISLAND

With my advance from this book, and some savings I had squirrelled away—plus some help from a couple of friends with very deep pockets—I bought that little island, and now visit it two to three times a year to pay my respects.

To what used to be. And to what could have been.

After the news broke, it became a worldwide news story due to the horror and mysteriousness of the events—not the least of which being how these people had all come to be trapped in a shipping container in the first place.

But besides that, if you ever wondered if cannibalism sells papers and ad space, the answer is: fucking right it does.

The first time I visited the island (a few months before I bought it, and not long after the police tape was taken down), you could still just make out Goatbaler's final sand-tweet. There were pictures of it all over the newspapers and websites—Goatbaler was right about that. Her tweet was, at the time, the most famous tweet in history.

Not many believed its claim, though, because after the police pieced together the events on the island, it became clear that she'd murdered more than her fair share of its inhabitants.

You can be woke AF, but the real world still takes shit like murder and cannibalism fairly seriously, so it sort of undercuts the credibility of your wild accusations once those charges are pinned on you.

When I found the tweet, I let it sit there in the sun for a little while. Then I moved one of my feet through it slowly, destroying it forever.

In its place, I wrote my own tweet in response:

DEAR WORLD,

ALEKSANDËR EATON IS NOT RESPONSIBLE FOR ANY OF THESE DEATHS. ALL WHO DIED HERE DESERVED THIS FATE. SOMEHOW, IT WAS MY REVENGE ON THEM FOR WHAT THEY DID TO ME. THEY CANCELLED ME, SO NOW I HAVE, QUITE LITERALLY, CANCELLED THEM. BUT WHAT I DID WAS FOR ALL OF YOU.

After the island became mine, and I began regularly visiting, I turned the refrigeration bunker (now cleared of any trace of corpses, of course) into a little tiki bar. For a laugh, I propped the Commandments up near the cash register, in between the rum and whiskey selections. (No one ever noticed that "Æ" was carved in very small letters on the back of one of the tablets. A shock to me, I must say, when I discovered it.)

I had a very small but well-appointed house built on the site where the castaways had made their main camp area. I left the Maersk shipping container where it was, though—it was just too weird and cool to get rid of.

I destroyed every safe space on the island, and now throw massive parties for grown-ups who realize that life owes them nothing.

The island has become my home away from home.

But my *true* home is still Marrakech, where:

—none of the mob's allegations were proven, nor any actual evidence given for these peoples' ridiculous attacks on my conduct. Simply a campaign of blind, jealous, woke-fuelled hatred, which drove this former hardcore left-winger firmly into the centre. If the goal is to lose allies and create political enemies, then cancel-culture mob justice is definitely the tool for the job.

—I sit on my porch and drink rum neat with a handful of true and trustworthy friends who stuck by me through that nightmare.

—I continue to write, to create, to work on new projects.

—I watch the events of five years ago recede more and more in my rearview mirror with every passing day.

One day, while sitting on the back patio at home in Marrakech, working on my new novel, there was a knock on the door. I put my laptop aside, went into the house, answered the door.

Mail had arrived. A little yellow package on the step.

I open it. It's a T-shirt from one of those friends who stuck by me.

I unfold the shirt, read what's written on the front.

I smile.

In massive white letters on a black background, it says:

STILL ALIVE, MOTHERFUCKER

aleksandereaton.substack.com

twitter.com/AleksanderEaton